# THE UN KNOWNS

## SHIRLEY-ANNE MCMILLAN

ATOM

ATOM

First published in Great Britain in 2017 by Atom

1 3 5 7 9 10 8 6 4 2

A CIP catalogue record for this book
is available from the British Library.

ISBN: 978-0-349-00253-8

Typeset in Garamond by M Rules
Printed and bound in Great Britain by
Clays Ltd, St Ives plc

Papers used by Atom are from well-managed forests
and other responsible sources.

Atom
An imprint of
Little, Brown Book Group
Carmelite House
50 Victoria Embankment
London EC4Y 0DY

An Hachette UK Company
www.hachette.co.uk

www.atom.co.uk

To Alex and Eoin

# THE UN KNOWNS

# Chapter 1

I could fall. I always knew I could fall. That was part of why I did it. Pulling up on rusty bars that could give way at any moment. Making my way to the top where there wasn't even dead metal to cling to; no safety barriers for people who were never meant to be up there in the first place; nobody to stop you jumping off. But up there was peace and silence, and the journey up was life and noise. Blood pulsing in your ears, the heart that knocks so hard you swear you can hear it out loud. How fast might I fall if I just let go now? How much would it hurt?

# Chapter 2

I was standing on Samson, looking down. I could see a fire. It sparked up, a tiny light in the distance. I sat down, cross-legged, on the wide floor of the tallest crane in Northern Ireland, its great arm holding me high above the town. In the black distance, the light of the fire was blossoming, yellow, like hope. But I could not feel its heat.

*Unless I jump*, I thought, *I am still really on the ground.*

But I wasn't planning to jump.

I let the cool air wrap itself around me. I wanted to stay there, where you could imagine things like falling off. Completely alone, but still attached.

But I knew I couldn't stay because if I did the morning would chase away the free feeling and I'd just be a girl who stayed out all night with no decent explanation. 'I wasn't with a boy, Dad, I was climbing up a crane.' Yeah, right. Nobody would believe Big Tilly was a climber. And that's the way I liked it. If Dad knew me properly he'd know that the crane explanation was far more likely than the boyfriend one, but that was Dad – always looking for scandal, even if it was never going to be true.

So I started to climb down. *Clump, clump, clump.* There is no graceful way to climb down a crane and I imagine that's true for those slim, lycra-clad climbers with their skinny legs as well.

Back to real life where everything is predictable and you know the next conversation is likely to be about school or studies. Back to 'reality', where you can't think out loud and where a bonfire is just a great big burning pile of wood.

But the next conversation was not about studies or school. In fact, it was unlike any conversation I had ever had before.

Nearing the ground, I saw it. Or, rather, I didn't see it. I had chained it up but I knew the lock wasn't great. My fault, I know. It should have been replaced ages ago. I slammed my feet on every rung – *bash bash bash* – I couldn't care who heard. It wasn't fair. The walk home would be an hour now and it would probably rain, and every climb I did from now on would be a hike as well as a climb. *Shit. Bash bash bash. Hope the feckers get hit by a bus. No I don't. Yes I do. Bash bash bash.*

On the ground I shone my torch into the space where I'd left my bike to get a closer look, and I noticed a shape moving and then someone stepped out of the shadow.

'Hey,' said the someone. 'Don't freak out.' He said it casually, like he regularly did this kind of thing, which made me even more nervous. 'Want some of this?' He held something out towards me. 'It's not drugs. Look.'

He cracked open the flask and poured something into the lid. The hot bitterness of it cut right through the freezing air. It was coffee. And yeah, I did want some. I didn't know what else was it in, though, or who this dude was, so I said no thanks. He shrugged and took a sip himself and then I didn't know what to do. I could have just walked off. I *should* have just walked off. But I guessed he'd probably have knifed me by now if he was going to, wouldn't he? And I needed to know something.

'Did you see who took my bike?'

'Someone took your bike? That's too bad.' His tone was flat but there was a hint of friendliness. Or maybe he was mocking me.

'Yeah. Come on, you must have seen something. I wasn't up there for long.'

He sipped the coffee and I wished I'd taken some. It smelt so good. I pulled my canvas jacket around me. He was leaning on the wall, where my bike had been, one foot on the bricks behind him, cool as you like. 'Climb much, do you?'

'Yeah ... why? Are you the cops?'

He involuntarily spat a mouthful of coffee out and wiped his gob with the back of his biker jacket. 'Naw! Do I look like a cop? Christ ...'

He looked at me with a grin; his eyes, ringed with eyeliner, were bright under the street lamp.

'Hey, seen enough?' he said, but he was still clearly amused. *Maybe he's not a he*, I thought. He sounded like a he. But he had a beautiful face that could be a girl's face. It was hard to tell with the make-up.

'Well, no offence,' I said, 'but I've no idea who you are. You turn up at the bottom of my climb, it's the middle of the night,

4

my bike is gone, and you ask me if I want some coffee. You have to admit it's a bit weird. And I find it hard to believe you never saw who took my bike.'

'Believe what you like. I'm a dealer, a stealer, a cop ... Maybe I'm just some guy out for a walk who saw someone at the top of a fuckin' massive crane and thought they were about to top themselves ...'

I could feel my face burn.

'So you thought you'd come over and watch? Have a little picnic?' I said.

'Aye. *Or* maybe I was thinking of climbing up to talk you down.'

Well, that shut me up. I've got to admit it, I really didn't know what to say then. Was he for real? Kids did kill themselves sometimes. Only last week it was someone from the school next to us. And when it happened you knew there'd be a couple more in the same area within a month or so. My gran used to tell me that during the Troubles people would watch the news at night to find out who'd been killed that day, and they'd sit there at the telly, praying it wasn't someone they knew, and then feeling guilty as hell because it was going to be someone that *somebody* knew and it was wrong to feel relief that it wasn't one of your own. No murders any more. Now we murder ourselves. Loads of schools have suicide prevention programmes, and maybe they help some people, but nobody really knows what to do about it. And I never heard of anyone climbing a crane to talk someone down, but maybe you would if you saw it. I couldn't think of what to say to him, but now I was curious. He hadn't stabbed me yet. So maybe ...

'Changed my mind,' I said. 'Can I have a bit of that coffee? It's bloody freezin'.'

He grinned and poured me a capful. It was scalding. I felt my nose start to run as I brought the cup to my mouth.

'So,' he said, as the coffee burned its way into my stomach, 'I swear to the little baby Jesus himself that I do not know which motherfucker stole your bike. I really was just out for a walk.'

'OK. Well, as you can see, I'm fine, and I appreciate the coffee and all, but I'll have to get going.'

He shrugged. 'Suit yourself. I was going to invite you to a party, but if you have to go . . .'

'What party?'

I was completely sure I wasn't going to go to a party in the middle of the night with a complete stranger, even if he was pretty good looking, even if I didn't want to go home. Did he think I was nuts?

'A good one,' he replied. *What a stupid thing to say*, I thought. But maybe it was a stupid question. I rolled my eyes, said thanks again for the coffee, and made to walk off.

'Hey!' he called. 'What's your name, Spider-Woman?'

It couldn't hurt to tell him my name, could it? It wasn't as if I'd ever see him again, and I didn't want to be rude.

'It's Tilly,' I called back as I continued to walk away. 'What's yours?'

'Brew. See you around, Tilly!' He waved and I turned back to my walk and raised a hand to wave back. I smiled to myself. *'See you around, Tilly.' Yeah, in my dreams, mate, and that's where I'd like you to stay.* The wind picked up and I drew my coat around myself as I tramped across the bridge to town.

A single ship moved across the black water and I fell in step with the rhythm of its little light, blinking. I felt the boards of the bridge, uneven, under my feet and cursed my stupidity in failing to get a new lock for my bike. Yet, angry as I was at myself, my mouth kept turning itself into a dumb grin as I went over his parting words. It was a moment to play with – a little thing that happened that I could call on the next time I felt like nothing would ever change. I wouldn't see him again. I was sure of that. *No problem, Brew; leave me to my boring life and my climbs and I'll see you again at the top of the next building when I'm on my own and it's safe to imagine you, and maybe in my mind we'll go to that party together too and who knows what could happen so far off the ground in the safety of my dreams. See you around, Brew, whoever you are.*

# Teen Gangs Continue Causing Trouble Across Belfast

# Chapter 3

'Tilly! Tilly? Come on, girl, it's almost 8 a.m. for God's sake!'

He yells the same thing every morning. I sat up and shoved my feet into my old trainers. You'd think he could vary the yelling a bit, just so the day started in a different way for once. It was the worst way to wake up. A constant reminder that nothing ever happened. Nothing interesting, anyway. I rubbed my eyes and remembered the climb from the night before and the day seemed slightly brighter.

'Come *on*. Are you up yet?' he continued to yell. 'And what the hell's your bike doing outside in the rain?'

What? I jumped up and pulled back the curtain. No way! There it was. My actual bike, casually sitting against the tree in our front garden, glittering with droplets of rain.

I ran downstairs, through the kitchen, past Dad pouring coffee and pulled on a raincoat.

'Hey – you need to get dressed! What's going on?'

'Don't stress, Dad,' I called from the hallway. 'I'm just going to get my bike.'

'But it . . .'

I shut the door behind me. The rain was light and cold and the birds sang through it. I checked my bike. No sign of damage. How on earth? And what was that?

I picked the soggy piece of paper out from between the spokes and looked around to make sure Dad hadn't seen from the window, but he wasn't there. I shoved the note in my pocket, dragged my bike over to the shed and pushed it in. The tube light on the shed ceiling buzzed and took a minute to light up and I brought out the note. It was written in capital letters and the ink was smudged because of the rain but I could still make it out. There was a number and a message.

IF YOU CHANGE YOR MIND ABOUT
THE PARTY GIV ME A CALL. BREW

Oh, wow. I mean, what? How did he get my bike? Maybe he'd hidden it? Maybe he'd been about to nick it and then saw me coming down and hid it? And how did he know where I lived? He must've followed me. What a creep! He'd stood there talking to me and swearing he knew nothing . . . urgh! But even though my brain knew that it was right to be angry, my mouth was smiling again. No way was I phoning him, of course. I wasn't a complete idiot. The guy was obviously some kind of hoodie nutter. And I'd have to be more careful about my little expeditions from now on . . . maybe I'd lie low for a couple of weeks . . . but . . . but nothing! This was totally unacceptable behaviour and it was totally dumb of me to feel anything but anger at this weirdo guy who was obviously some kind of stalker and . . .

*Duff. Duff. Duff.*

I opened the shed door to see my dad banging on the kitchen window and pointing to his watch. Shit – he was actually right this time – I was going to be late. I put the note in my pocket and ran inside. And that was the thing that changed everything: not the climb, or meeting Brew for the first time, not drinking his coffee or telling him my name. Putting that note in my pocket – that's what made it all happen. I knew I should've torn it up straight away. But I didn't. I kept it, just in case of something that I didn't know yet, and that something would happen later that day and suddenly that free part of my life that I saved for being up in the air would come closer to the ground than I ever could have imagined.

# Chapter 4

I dialled the number. It rang. I hung up.

Four times in a row.

There is a part of me which will always be my dad: sensible, clever, organised, knowing what to do. But it isn't all of me; that's the problem. The rest of me is connected to the me that I can be when I climb. But I keep the two me's quite separate and the me that was dialling the number on Brew's note would never do something like this. But I had to know. I was angry with him but I was curious too, and I was bored. I didn't want it to end with his note going in the bin, if I'm honest. Him asking my name, me asking his, finding the note on my bike. Those moments were like a little match being struck in a dull room. But they would burn out eventually and the room would be grey again. I wanted more.

I dialled again. Last time, I told myself. If I can't follow it through then that is that – my dad's voice wins – and maybe it's for the best. But he answered before it rang three times.

'Tilly?'

'How did you know it was me? Or did you steal my phone number as well last night?'

He laughed.

'Naw. I guessed. And I didn't steal your bike.'

'Bullshit. And how did you know where I live?'

'Hey, are you angry? I brought your bike back!'

'Yeah, but you so obviously took it in the first place. And there's the small matter of you totally stalking me . . . '

'I did not! Well, OK, I did kind of follow you a little bit . . . '

'A little . . . ?'

'But I didn't take your bike. I swear.'

'Oh what, you just happened to find it as you were following me home, then?'

'Kind of. Not really. I will explain . . . but not right now. And I'm sorry I followed you, but I kind of had to, to give your bike back. I thought you'd be pleased!'

'I'm slightly freaked out if you must know.'

'I can tell!' He laughed again. 'Look, Tilly. I'm nobody, right? If you tell me to piss off now, I will. You won't see me or hear from me again. I totally promise. I'm not a stalker and I'm not trying to freak you out. If you must know, I like you.'

I could feel my face heat up and I held the phone away from my mouth so I could take a breath without him hearing. How was I meant to respond to that? Maybe I should hang up now. I'd got my match-flame moment. But I didn't hang up. The silence was only seconds but it seemed to go on for ages.

'You still there?' he asked.

'Yeah.'

'Well?'

'Well what?'

'Well, say something. I don't know!' He laughed again.

'I ... I don't know what to say. I don't really know you. And you don't know me. How could you like me?'

'I don't know many girls who climb up cranes in the middle of the night.'

It was my turn to laugh.

'That's better,' he said. 'You have a nice laugh, Tilly.'

The match-flame made my face burn again.

'You missed a great party last night,' he continued. 'There's another one in a while. You should come.'

'Brew. I don't think I should go to a party with you. It was nice, I mean weird but in a nice way, to meet you and everything, and ... thank you for bringing my bike back, if that's what happened, but I'm not going to go to some random party with you.'

'OK. Then meet me. You free later? Around 7 p.m.?'

I was. Dad was working late. I was meant to be studying but he totally trusted me. He wouldn't try to check up. I could easily slip out. But did I want to? Yes, I really did.

'Yeah, OK.'

'OK. How about down at the docks again – at the Ark? You can get me a coffee this time.'

'OK. I'll see you then. And you'd better have a good story for how you "found" my bike.'

'Oh yeah? What if I don't?'

'Well then, the coffee's on you.' I could tell we were both grinning at one another down the phone. Dad-me was so far away. I didn't even know I could be flirtatious in real life, but

16

I guess the person you are inside your head sometimes can be who you really are as well. It was so bold, though – to meet a stranger. I hung up, set down the phone, and as I did I noticed my hand shaking slightly. I could climb a crane or a bridge or a building with no harness and stand at the top, cool as you like, balanced above the city. But here I was in my own kitchen, using two hands to fill the kettle in case I dropped it. This wasn't me. But it was me. And nobody knew it. Nobody but me and Brew. I wondered how dangerous those match-flames might be if a shaking hand should drop one.

# Chapter 5

He was sitting outside at one of the Ark Cafe's wooden picnic tables, smoking a fag with an espresso cup in front of him, his army surplus jacket buttoned up to the neck. When he saw me he gave me a nod of greeting and smiled with half his mouth. He stubbed out the fag.

'Wanna go inside? It's a bit windy out here.'

It looked like he'd decided already but he was right – it was cold and, besides, there were more people inside so it felt more sensible. I wanted to keep as close to sensible-me as possible . . .

'This OK?' He indicated a table and I nodded. He ordered another espresso and I must have raised an eyebrow.

'Serious addiction.' He grinned. 'You?'

'Me what?'

'What's your vice?'

'I don't really have any, er, vices.'

'I guess it's dangerous enough climbing up cranes with no safety net, eh?'

He was so sure of himself. It was hard not to like that about him. But I didn't want to talk about myself. I ordered a tea.

'So. My bike.'

'Ha! OK. Here's the story. I didn't see who did it, but' – he sipped his espresso – 'I did have a fair idea of who it might be.'

'Why didn't you tell me?'

'Cos. No point. I knew I could get it back if it was him.'

'Who? And why did you get it back anyway? What's it to you?'

'Told you. I like you.'

This time he could see my face redden. He grinned and I tried to hide my face by taking an enormous gulp of tea, which burned my mouth badly, but I couldn't spit it out so I had to swallow and it made me choke and splutter, which made me feel even more stupid. Of course, he found it hilarious.

'Heh! Sorry. Didn't mean to freak you out again.'

'You're loving this!'

'I am a bit.'

'Anyway,' I said, trying to regain my dignity, 'so who nicked my bike, and what, did they just hand it back to you? Are you some kind of gang leader or something?'

It was a crap joke but he seemed to find it very amusing indeed.

'Seany nicked your bike. He's a mate of mine. We're in the same, well, "gang", I suppose.'

'Nice mates you have.' I raised an eyebrow.

Seriously, what was I doing? Yes, this guy was cute, and his eyeliner underscored the bluest eyes I'd ever seen, and the way he hunched over his espresso made it seem like he was the oldest teenager in the world, and he seemed so cheerful, like nothing could possibly be a problem to him . . . but he was still a stranger, and apparently one with criminal mates. I looked at my phone. 20.12. If I hadn't met Brew I'd've had an hour of study done by now. I'd be immersed in 'The Pardoner's Tale', not finding out about Belfast's criminal underworld. I can just imagine Dad's reaction. 'Scumbag hoodies', he'd call them – the kind of 'feckless, lazy' kids who'd steal a person's bike without a minute's thought. I looked up at Brew. He wasn't smiling any more. Fiddling with his espresso cup, he didn't lift his eyes as he spoke.

'Seany is OK. He's . . . kind of mixed up.'

He looked up at me, his face still serious.

'I'm sorry he took your bike. He shouldn't've. I had a go at him for it and he didn't put up an argument. You'd probably like him if you met him.'

'Huh. I don't think *that*'s going to happen.'

'Yeah, well.' He finished off his espresso. 'I know that, really. We – I mean, our group – we're kind of different . . . I just thought that you . . . because of climbing the crane and everything . . . I thought you might like us . . . I thought you seemed a bit different too.'

*I am different!* I wanted to say. *I'm different to everyone! That's why I have to climb stuff – I can't even be myself when I'm on the ground!* But I didn't say it. I just finished my tea. And it was silent then and I thought that probably that was it. We'd finish up, go home and the encounter would be dead – the match burned out for good.

But that's not what happened. What happened was that the

Ark Cafe's door opened and a woman wearing a headscarf and sunglasses came in. It was 20.45 now and raining and she was dressed like someone who was about to get into a convertible sports car and drive across America.

'Ah. Wait here,' said Brew. 'If you want to, that is.'

I did want to. Brew got up and went over to the woman. As he spoke to her she lifted her sunglasses slightly and looked over at me like she was checking me out. I wondered what he was telling her. She was too old to be a girlfriend . . . or his mum . . . and she didn't look like a grandmother . . . After about five minutes she nodded and the two of them embraced. She kissed Brew on both cheeks and left the cafe.

'That was Meg,' he said, sitting down again.

'Is she in your gang too?' I joked.

'Yep.'

'What? Seriously?'

He was back to smiling again, but he wasn't going to give much away.

'Want another tea?'

I looked at the time on my phone. There was a missed call from Dad. Shit.

'No, sorry. I have to go.'

'Another time, maybe?'

I looked out at the rain and zipped my coat up. I really hoped that Dad wasn't going to go spare. At least I'd have the journey home to figure out what to tell him. I looked at Brew, tracing his finger around the rim of his espresso cup. I did want to see him again. This had been the most interesting evening I'd had for ages. He *was* different and I wanted to know more about his gang of people who nicked bikes and then gave them back and old ladies who dressed like they were from the 1950s. But it was probably a bad idea. Sensible-me said to leave it there – I'd had a bit of fun, but I had exams to think about.

'I don't think so, Brew. It was nice meeting you, though.'

But even as I said it, I wasn't completely sure that I would never see him again. Belfast wasn't that big. Anything could happen, couldn't it?

# Chapter 6

Dad had been waiting for me at home, of course. He had decided to bring some work home with him. He didn't go spare after all, but he did want to know where I'd been. I told him I'd just gone out for some fresh air.

'Yes, well. I suppose fresh air will help with the revision,' he said. Typical. One-track frickin' mind. But at least he was actually in favour of fresh air. And it meant I could go out again some time. If I wanted to, which obviously I didn't . . .

I took off my wet coat and boots. They were dripping all over the floor.

'In the shower,' said Dad without looking up from his laptop.

'Eh?'

'Put your wet stuff in the shower.'

He looked up and took off his glasses.

'You're soaked,' he said. 'The water's hot – maybe put yourself in the shower first.'

He was trying to be nice. Dad was OK really. He was so strict about school and about how my future was going to turn out, but I knew that it was only because he wanted me to be OK.

'What are you writing about?' I asked, holding my coat over the sink. He sighed and rubbed his eyes before putting his glasses back on and looking back to the screen. He squinted at the words and hit the space bar a couple of times.

'It's a story about these kids who've been arsing about and messing things up.'

'What kids?'

'Oh, a bunch of hoodies – the usual. But this is the second time the same group have been involved in an incident.' He hit backspace several times and adjusted a couple of words. 'This time they were involved in a racist incident in Roden Street.'

'Oh, I heard about that! Some guy was getting harassed because he was Russian.'

'Ukrainian.' He continued to delete and adjust as he spoke. 'Yes, this mob of hoodies have been caught up with it all. Same lot as the ones who were in the middle of that riot last week. Looks like we have a gang problem in Belfast again.'

The word 'gang' made me catch my breath.

'Are there any pictures of them?'

Dad took off his glasses to look at me again. He sat back in his seat and looked me in the eyes.

'No. There are no photographs of them. Have you heard anything about them in school or anything? Are kids talking about them?'

'No!' I might have said it too loudly. I hated it when Dad did this. He was always trying to get the 'youth' angle on stories about young people. I don't know why on earth he ever thought I might know anything. He knew how completely dull my life was.

'OK, OK. Just, em, let me know if you do hear anything, OK? The more we know about these thugs the quicker the police can deal with them.'

'And then you'd have nothing to write about, eh?' I smiled at him to make sure he knew I was joking as I lifted my boots and coat. But it was only a half joke. Dad was an OK guy really – I knew that because I lived with him and because he cooked dinner most of the time and tried to make sure I behaved myself. But I didn't like his paper, with its obsession with 'young people today' – it was so judgemental, as if people my dad's age never smoked or went out drinking when they were teenagers. I knew that my climbing adventures would make a great story for them and that they'd probably twist it into some kind of wrongness.

As the hot water hit my skin and the warmth coursed over me, I decided that I should definitely never see Brew again. I didn't know for sure that his gang were the group my dad was writing about, but they might as well be. And if my dad ever found out that I'd been meeting up with a 'hoody'– let alone one with eye make-up and decidedly weird friends – then that would be the end of my climbing adventures because he'd be watching over me 24/7. And I needed to climb. Much more than I needed a boyfriend, or a girlfriend . . . so that was it. I scrubbed my hair with too much shampoo and the suds dropped in huge puddles. Climbing was how I knew myself, how I knew my body, and I couldn't let anything or anybody take me away from it. I took out his note from under my mattress and tore into little pieces.

# Chapter 7

Shopping, unless it's shopping for books, is really my idea of hell. Walking miles around the high street with loads of people in your face and walking into shops with smiley assistants who want to 'help' you and looking at rails and rails of clothes that you hate . . . urgh. No thanks. But Beth wanted to go shopping and Dad was letting me off Saturday afternoon study, because he likes Beth. She is 'a good influence' in every way; bright, hard-working, top of everything in every class, gorgeous. Even her chestnut hair is well behaved – straight and sleek – her fringe cut in a sharp line. She was everything Dad thought a young lady should be. He never ever said 'Why can't you be more like Beth?' but he thought it quite loudly sometimes.

Anyway, she sounds like a pain, but actually it was impossible not to like Beth. It wasn't her fault she was like Mary Poppins – *practically perfect in every way* – she was also funny and kind and a good friend. When Mum died she was one of the only kids who didn't feel so awkward around me that they stopped talking to me.

'What about this one?'

Beth was holding a green vest top against her chest.

'Is it too slutty?'

'Nah,' I said. 'Be slutty if you want to be.'

She opened her mouth in mock horror and I giggled.

'Seriously, though,' I said, 'that colour is rank. It looks like bogeys.'

'Really? Oh God,' she said, looking at it again. 'Yes, you're right!'

I laughed again. Beth was as bad at shopping as me, but somehow she still enjoyed it.

'Are you bored?' she said, placing the snotty top back on the rack. 'Shall we go for coffee?'

'You know me so well!'

Beth took my arm and we headed for the door. No need to ask which coffee place we were going to – we always went to the same one. Delaney's. The only coffee place in town that hadn't turned into an American chain place, and therefore the only one where we knew we could avoid all the other kids from school on a Saturday.

Delaney's was dark as usual. We sat in a booth being careful not to bang our heads on the Tiffany lamps that hung low over the table. The waitress came over.

'The usual?'

'Yes please.'

'I don't know how you stay so skinny,' she said to Beth, who blushed on my behalf.

She wrote down our order: two mocha shakes and a banana split to share. Sugar-hit heaven.

'Actually, make it a banana split each today,' I said, winking at Beth. 'Poor Beth needs the calories.'

Beth giggled but it was lost on the waitress, who amended the order and smiled sincerely before walking off, her apron strings waving from side to side against her ample bum.

I thought about telling Beth about Brew. She could keep a secret – I knew that. She'd never told anyone that I kissed Shauneen Jackson behind the gym at school two years ago. Well, some other people knew, because they'd dared us both to do it, but nobody except Beth knew that I had quite enjoyed the experience. We could talk endlessly about stuff like that and I knew she'd never tell a soul. All the same, I hadn't told her about climbing. Not because I didn't trust her, but because that was just for me. I wasn't ready to let anyone else into that side of me. But maybe I could tell her about Brew? I wasn't sure.

It was so dark and cosy in here. Our drinks and desserts arrived. The waitress smiled.

'I put extra chocolate sauce on the ice cream. You might as well!'

'Thanks,' said Beth, sparkling. Everyone liked her, even when she was just ordering a milkshake. I'd never be like that. But maybe that was OK. I grabbed a spoon. As soon as the waitress was gone, Beth put both hands palm down on the table and looked me directly in the eyes.

'OK, so,' she began. She was all smiles and I was all ears. She looked like she was going to announce her engagement or something.

'What? What's happened?'

'I met a boy!'

Uh-oh. Beth enjoyed boy shopping as much as she enjoyed clothes shopping, and her taste was just as good. Still, I was glad that I didn't have to decide whether or not to tell her about Brew because for the next forty minutes she talked incessantly about someone called Daniel and I heard all about where she'd met him (tennis club), how fit he was (tennis skills *and* biceps) and how he 'wasn't like all the other guys' (nobody ever was. Except they always were). She jabbered on about how she was sure he was on the verge of asking her out and how she wasn't sure about it because he was older than her (he was eighteen) and had an earring, and that maybe the earring suggested he was the rebellious sort and although she had nothing against rebels maybe it meant that he wouldn't be entirely committed to her and she didn't want to have a serious break-up in the middle of her A levels. Good grief. They hadn't even kissed yet and she was planning the break-up.

'What do you think, Tilly? Does he sound too ... alternative?'

I choked on my mocha shake.

'Because he has an earring? No, Beth, I don't think he sounds too wild.'

'You can laugh, Tilly, but I need to be sensible. Or do I? Maybe I need to take a risk?'

Suddenly the conversation was interesting.

I scooped some of the melting ice cream and pointed my spoon at Beth.

'You need to have some fun, Beth. It's me that needs to be sensible. You can afford to get out a bit. You're top of everything.'

'It's only because I work so hard,' she said, squirming slightly at the suggestion.

'It's not. I work as hard as you and I can't get your grades. You can relax a bit!'

'Oh my God, Tilly, you're like the little devil on my shoulder whispering badness into my ear!'

I laughed, but I knew what she meant. I hadn't been able to stop thinking about Brew, even though I really wanted to leave him behind in the Ark Cafe.

'Look, you're racing too far ahead of everything. Think about what's real: he's a guy that you like and you think he likes you too. If he asks you out you can go out with him once – it doesn't mean you're planning your whole life or anything. You can just take things as they come. Find out about him. Maybe he's in the Ra. But he's probably just a bloke with an earring.'

Beth sipped the end of her mocha shake and shook her head.

'You're so wise, Tilly! I keep thinking that everything I do has, like, eternal consequences, or something. But you're right. If I met him for a coffee it would just be a coffee, wouldn't it?'

I shrugged my shoulders. 'Sure.' Yeah, it was just a coffee. Wasn't it?

We finished up and left the cafe, the sun blinding us as we opened the door and set out again on the high street. Beth wanted to get shopping again; now that she'd decided to meet Daniel, should he ask her out, she needed something to wear, and I needed to steer her away from anything that should be caught in a hankie and chucked in the bin. We headed into the heart of the high street, buzzing with people talking and laughing, kids screaming, boys in tracksuits shouting across the street to girls in short skirts standing outside McDonald's.

Beth had my arm firmly in hers again as she chatted on and on about Daniel and his brown eyes and his job in the civil service. Underneath the noise of the city I could hear singing in the distance. A busker, singing an unusual song. The slow-picked guitar could barely be heard beneath his voice. I recognised the words. It was from *West Side Story*. We'd done it in school the year before. It was a song about wanting to find a place to belong when everything seemed against you.

I found myself drawn towards it. I knew it was him. The voice was so warm, and I wanted to hear it all, even if he saw me, even if it was against the plan.

'Hey, where are you going? Next is this way . . . '

'I just want to hear this song.'

Beth rolled her eyes but she was just kidding. She followed me and as the song grew louder the crowd became smaller and we found ourselves standing there in front of him as he sang the final words.

Brew grinned at me and Beth, who had been standing with one hand on her heart, broke into applause.

'Oh wow, Tilly!' she whispered to me. 'He's amazing!'

'I know,' I said.

'And he's gorgeous too.'

*I know*, I thought.

Brew did a formal bow towards Beth and she threw a pound coin in his guitar case.

'Many thanks!' he said to her, but he was looking at me.

I don't believe in fate, I really don't. But so what if I met him again? Just once? Nothing bad had happened. I wouldn't let anything bad happen. I could make decisions as I went along. Good decisions. I wouldn't get mixed up in anything bad. I could just meet him one more time. Didn't I deserve some fun too?

'Beth, stay here. I just need the loo. I'll be right back.'

She was happy to stay as Brew started up again. This time a rockier number. I listened to his song in time with my steps as I ducked into the nearest shop and found a dark corner to take out my notebook.

*Lost your number. Call me. If you want to*, I wrote.

By the time I got back to Beth she was clapping in time to a Beatles song and a small crowd had gathered to listen. I wrapped my note around a pound coin and dropped it into Brew's guitar case. He winked at me as he carried on singing and I grabbed Beth and led her away before I could change my mind and fish the note out again.

'What's the big rush? And what did you put in his case?'

'What? Em, nothing! Just a quid.'

'Lies!' she screamed, laughing. 'Did you just give him your number? Oh my GOD you did!'

She squealed in delight and led me off to the shop she'd been looking for, gabbling away about how brazen I was and how she wished she had my confidence and of course I had to tell her if he called and everything he said. I promised her I would but I knew that I probably wouldn't tell her everything, and I thought about being on top of Samson and my bike going missing, about the Ark and Meg, and about how far away from normal life my secrets had taken me and might take me yet.

# Chapter 8

It was a week later and I was at the top of the derelict court-house on the Crumlin Road when my phone rang. I'd been leaning out and peering over the edge when the tone sounded. It made me jump and I had one of those moments that shakes me out of my solitary mode. If I'd been any closer to the edge . . . I should turn my phone off when I do a climb. I don't like being disturbed. It was probably Dad. I went to switch my phone off. Dad can never get in on my climbs. I love him, but he isn't invited, even over the phone.

But it wasn't Dad's number. It rang and rang as I took deep breaths and considered whether to answer. In the end I decided it was OK. Brew had disturbed my climbs once before and it hadn't ruined this one to know that he knew about them. We were still strangers, really. It was OK to let a stranger in, right? It was only a phone call and, anyhow, he wouldn't be able to tell I was on a climb . . .

'Hi. Is that Brew?'

'It is. How's the view up there?'

I almost dropped the phone.

'Up where? How did you . . . '

'On top of the courts. I'm here. I can see you.'

'What??'

I looked out over the edge again. A small light was waving from the ground and it called out, 'Yooooo hooooo!' I put the phone to my ear again.

'Sssssh! Shut up, you dick, you'll get me caught.'

'Doubt it. No cops around tonight and nobody else cares that you're on top of a ruined building.'

'What . . . what are you doing here? Did you follow me?'

'Come on, Tilly. I don't follow you around all the time. *You* gave *me* your number this time, remember?'

I didn't know if I could believe him. This part of the city was so quiet. That's why I chose it. He was right about the lack of cops. Another reason why I was here. It was my first climb since meeting him at Samson. He hadn't called for days and I thought that was it – he'd changed his mind – and I'd been trying not to care because I had studies to do and I thought he was arrogant anyway . . . but to be honest I'd been going nuts wondering why he hadn't called. So I'd decided to go out on a climb to clear my head and refocus, and it had been working. I'd been enjoying looking out over another part of the city, imagining the people asleep in their beds, wondering who they were and where they worked. I had hardly thought about Brew at all until the phone rang.

'You still there, Tilly?'

'Yeah. I'm coming down. Hang on.'

As I climbed down the rusty fire escape on the side of the

building, my heart was thumping and I couldn't decide if it was excitement or annoyance. Probably both. I didn't want my climbs to be interrupted like this. I needed them to be mine. On my own. Some of the rungs were missing so I had to cling to the sides of the ladder while I put my weight on the next rung to make sure it wasn't going to give way. It was slow, but I liked that. Derelict buildings would let you climb them if you treated them with respect. I jumped off the last unbroken rung, about three feet from the ground, and landed with a thud beside Brew.

'My bike's still here!'

He laughed.

'Yep. I was guarding it.'

'No coffee tonight, then?' I smiled. It turned out that I was glad to see him after all.

'You want some? Or maybe a beer?'

I looked around where he stood. He had no bag with him and it was at least 1 a.m. Everywhere would be shut.

'I wasn't following you,' he said. 'You followed me.'

'Eh?'

'Come on.'

Brew turned his back and beckoned me to follow. We walked around to the back and over to the furthest corner of the building. I could see a small light glowing and as we got closer it was clear that the window was broken. Brew stepped through and turned to me.

'You coming?'

I wasn't sure. Was this where he lived? I didn't know if I liked the idea. I still didn't really know him. And then there was a voice from inside. A Northern Irish accent, but posh, like a newsreader on the telly.

'Brew? Is that you, darling? Did you bring milk?'

'Naw, sorry,' he called back to the voice. 'I'll get it later. I brought something better!'

'Who's that?' I said.

'It's Meg. You remember – from the cafe? Come on, it's warmer in here and I want you meet everyone. We can trust you, right?'

I didn't know if he could trust me. Him and his gang of hoodies. I expected that the guy who stole my bike was in there too. What were they doing? Taking drugs? That Meg hadn't seemed like a druggie, though. Brew sighed.

'OK, look. I'll bring them out here. You can say hi and then go home if you like. I suppose I can't blame you for being scared.'

'I'm not scared!'

But Brew had disappeared into the dark ruin. I thought about taking off right then. Heading home. Deleting his number, again. But I stayed. Because to be honest I was curious, and I did kind of trust him. He had brought my bike back. And it was true, he hadn't hassled me. Maybe I could just find out who they all were. And then I could decide for sure about that coffee.

# Chapter 9

Assembled in the dark, on the grass behind the old ruined courthouse, there were five of them, including Meg and Brew.

Brew introduced them, pointing to each one as he said their name.

'Tilly, this is Meg – our glorious leader.' Meg, older, tall and glamorous with a patterned shawl draped around her bony shoulders, scowled at him. 'Just kidding, Meg.' He grinned.

'And this' – he pointed to a small scrawny-looking kid with glasses who was hugging his bare arms against the cold – 'this is Seany.'

It was my turn to scowl. Seany gave a nervous wave.

'Sorry I took your bike,' he said. 'I just . . . saw it there and thought someone had abandoned it . . .'

'It was locked up!'

'Um, yeah. Sorry . . .' He stepped back into the shadow and Brew, smiling as if he thought it was hilarious, continued.

'Scar,' he said, pointing to a guy, definitely a guy, maybe about twenty-five years old, with a beard, and a broad chest, wearing a dress. I raised an eyebrow. I didn't mean to be rude – it just kind of happened. I'd never seen a big bearded man wearing a flowery dress before. I looked at him, hopeful that I hadn't offended him and he smiled a broad grin showing the whitest and most straight teeth I'd ever seen.

'Hello, Tilly!' He beamed. 'Welcome to our little group.'

His voice was warm and open and I liked him straight away. It made me wonder how good my character judgement was, because he was yet another stranger, but I knew I wanted to know him better.

'Thanks.' I smiled back. Brew went on with his introductions. He indicated a small girl who looked like she might've been the same age as me. 'This is Sara,' said Brew. She smiled shyly and raised a hand in welcome.

'Everyone,' Brew said, 'this is Tilly. She's a climber, she's pretty cool, and she has no idea what to make of us. So I'm proposing we take her out on tonight's mission. What do you all think?' Brew turned to me. 'Will you come in, Tilly? It's warmer and we're OK, honest.'

I looked at the group and they did seem OK. Weird, but not dangerous. I wasn't sure about any 'mission' but I reminded myself that I could just go home if I wanted. And surely I could trust the guy in the dress. He had such a kind face. I nodded and everyone smiled, glad to return to whatever lay inside the old crumbling building.

# Chapter 10

Inside the old courthouse it was warmer and brighter than I expected. We got to the room after we'd gone down a couple of corridors (which were dark. Really dark. I wanted to grab on to someone, but not Brew, so I stumbled behind him, doing my best with my phone light.) The room that we ended up in seemed lived-in. They must have been hanging out here for a while. *It's a squat*, I thought. *They're homeless.*

'Welcome,' said Brew. 'Take a seat, wherever.'

It was the walls I noticed first. The room wasn't much bigger than our living room but the walls were covered in colourful graffiti which made it seem smaller. Bold writing – song lyrics or poetry – and designs like huge mad doodles and cartoon people with names underneath them. In the centre of the wall facing me was a large black circle with the letter 'A' in red in the middle. I'd seen it on some kids' schoolbags. I didn't really know what it meant except that those kids were usually the ones who got detention. You could hardly see the white of the walls beneath all the colour.

'You like it?'

'Did you do it?' I asked.

'We all did, darling,' said Meg, sweeping herself onto a large cushion. 'Come! Have a seat!'

She patted the cushion beside her and raised both eyebrows. So I sat. And everyone else sat too. We were in a semi-circle facing a glowing gas radiator. There was a large standard lamp in the corner of the room but it wasn't plugged in. Instead there was a huge torch lashed to the bit where the bulb should be. Candles lit the rest of the room.

Scar spoke first.

'Well, firstly – welcome to Tilly!'

Everyone stared at me and most of them smiled. Meg patted my back and leant in towards my ear. 'These are good people,' she whispered. 'They mean their welcome.'

'Now,' Scar went on. He was sitting on three cushions, his big boots crossed beneath the long dress which covered his knees. 'Tilly's new and she doesn't know anything about us, really – that's right, isn't it, Tilly?'

I nodded.

'But unfortunately, time is against us tonight because according to Barra it's going to rain later.'

I glanced at Brew.

'Barra Best. The weather man off telly,' he explained.

'So, I'm sorry, Tilly,' Scar said, 'but Brew's going to have to explain things as we travel tonight, cos if we're going we need to do it soon. OK?'

I had no idea if that was OK. Going where? And they were talking to me like I was part of their group now. I really hoped they didn't think I was part of their gang.

'OK,' I said.

'Is that OK with everyone else?' Scar said.

'If Tilly's here it's because Brew trusts her,' said Meg, placing a hand warmly on my shoulder again. 'That's good enough for me.'

'Me too,' said Seany, not meeting my eyes.

'And me,' said Sara.

Scar nodded and the discussion quickly moved on. I was in. I had no idea what that meant, but they had decided to trust me.

'So what's the deal, then?' Seany said to Scar.

'Meg, you tell us – you're the one who knows most about it.' Scar looked at Meg and she stretched out her legs in front of her and leant back, her hands behind her on the floor. If she really was in her seventies you wouldn't know it. She looked completely comfortable sitting on the floor, stretched out like a child watching TV.

'OK, love. Well. Some delightful individuals have taken it upon themselves to decorate Mackin's play park on the Ormeau Road with a little note of welcome for the local children. I took some pictures on my way here this evening.'

Meg handed round the phone and I swiped the pictures one by one:

*NO TAIGS HERE.* (White paint, large letters on the back wall of the park near the swings.)

*KAT.* (Which means 'Kill All Taigs'– also on the back wall.)

*FUCK OFF TAIGS.* (Red, white and blue paint, massive letters, on the wall near the sand pit.)

The group was silent for a minute, their faces solemn. Some looked at the floor.

41

'Does this even need discussion?' Brew said.

Silence again.

'OK then,' said Scar. 'I think we should get down there quick as we can and get to work. Anyone object to that?'

Everyone shook their heads.

'OK then,' said Brew. 'Let's hit the road. Sara and Scar, how about youse lead the way? I'll hang back with Tilly here and fill her in. See you all back here after?'

And so I left the building, towards some unknown 'mission', with this weird gang of people who you wouldn't have put together in the real world: Scar-in-the-dress alongside mousy Sara; super-posh Meg, old-and-not-old; Brew-who-likes-me-but-doesn't-call. It was only Seany who I hadn't warmed to and maybe it was natural to be annoyed by someone who had stolen your bike. Somehow, although they were all strangers, and strange strangers at that, I knew I wasn't afraid of them.

# Chapter 11

'So, it's like this.'

We walked in darkness. Phone lights had to be switched off. We had to look like just a group of people walking home from somewhere. Casual. Quiet. Sara and Scar, then Meg and Seany behind them, and lastly me and Brew, who was telling me all about the group.

'We meet whenever we meet – there's no set time or anything. Everyone's got a phone anyway so it's easy to gather at the courthouse. Sometimes to do a mission, sometimes just to hang out.'

'Oh, I thought you all lived at the courthouse,' I said.

'You thought Meg lives at the courthouse?' He smirked.

'Well ... I don't know ...'

'Nah. I'm the only one who lives there. It's a good place to meet.'

'OK, well, what do you mean, missions? Like stealing bikes?'

'Heh. No.'

'Then what?'

'Well, different things. You'll see tonight.'

'Is it . . . is it illegal stuff?'

He laughed again and took a drag of his cigarette.

'Sometimes, yeah. But in a good way.'

I had no idea what he meant and I was pretty sure my dad wouldn't understand him either. We were getting near to the park and I was already making plans for how to slip away.

'Hey.' Brew nudged me. 'Cheer up. We're not Nazis or anything.'

I smiled.

'Druggies, I was thinking, actually.'

He laughed hard and I laughed too. But I wasn't really joking. My dad would kill me if he knew where I was right now and who with. And who *was* I with, anyway? I still really knew nothing about any of them, except that Brew was homeless.

'We're not druggies,' he said, stamping out his cigarette butt on the pavement. 'Well, apart from me and these bloody things. But no, none of us light up anything stronger than that, I promise.'

'Am I . . .' I wanted to ask it, but it felt silly, like something a child would ask in a primary school playground.

'Are you . . . what?' he said.

I took a breath.

'Am I . . . I mean, have I joined something? Am I in your group now?'

'Do you want to be?'

'No. I mean, I don't know. I still don't really know what it's all about.'

'Well, it's up to you. You can be with us or not. You can go home tonight and never see us again. Up to you. I won't follow you home again, if that's what you're worried about.'

He was teasing.

'No, I'm not worried about that.'

'Oh, so I *can* follow you home?'

I laughed, glad that he couldn't see my face, hot in the dark. I've always been useless at flirting. I could hear Beth telling me to 'get in there' and say something witty back, but I couldn't think of anything at all. I could see her in my mind rolling her eyes. I could see the park and I was glad that we were almost there because I was afraid that in the dark Brew might reach out and grab my hand. And part of me wished that he would. But he didn't, and then we were there, and Scar was turning around with his finger to his mouth telling us all to keep quiet and handing out spray cans.

# Chapter 12

On weekends my dad let me lie in a bit, but that morning I had set my alarm to make me get up at a reasonable 'lie in' time so he wouldn't suspect how late I had come in. It went off at 11 a.m. and I made myself climb out of bed and go down to the kitchen. The night before was knocking at my head, wanting to parade in and dance around all day, replaying what we did and what happened and where we went. But I shut it out. I'd think about it later when I was on my own and didn't have to play the part of a normal daughter, making toast and tea and pretending that my life hadn't suddenly just got *really* interesting.

Dad was drinking coffee in his suit and tutting loudly at the laptop, no doubt gearing up to go to work and write his outraged spin on what he was reading.

'Morning, Tills,' he said, looking up.

'Morning.' I clicked the bread down into the toaster and went looking for the jam.

Dad tapped the mouse.

'Young louts at it again!'

I almost dropped the butter knife.

'What do you mean?'

I knew what he meant. He read the email aloud. 'Police brief: Gang of Unknowns Targets Kiddie Play Park'

He shook his head and I turned my back to him so he couldn't see my panic. He didn't notice though.

'Seems this group of thugs just can't leave anything alone! The police almost caught them, but not quite.'

The story of last night was shoving at the door in my mind. I heard Brew's voice, low and urgent: '*Run.*' And we did run, all the way back to the courts. We didn't stop until we got there. The cops were miles away by then.

'Do they know who it is?' I asked, trying to spread jam without my hand shaking.

'Nah. Little gits got away. Again. But it won't be long before they do. They've built up quite a file on these little twerps. I'll probably get Cartwright to cover this story, but I'm thinking of doing a feature on their activities in general. Maybe get the public to be on the lookout . . . For goodness' sake, Tilly, watch what you're doing!'

I had dropped the knife again.

'Sorry, Dad. Butterfingers!'

He tutted and went back to his emails.

I knew I couldn't eat the toast but also that I couldn't put it in the bin in front of Dad, so I took it and the tea to my room, the memory of last night finally bursting through as I lay down on my bed and went through it all. It had happened. I had been there. And now it was going to be in the papers. And Dad was going to do a story on the gang.

As soon as Scar had given out the cans of spray paint they went to work, quickly, silently. Brew beckoned me to follow him and we want to the side of the park. The swings moved gently in the dark, lit only by street lights at the gate. The climbing frame and slide were giant sleeping shadows, unaware of the work going on around them. The cans hissed. Brew covered his mouth and nose with his T-shirt. He was blotting out the sectarian words in smooth clean strokes, making a blank canvas. Everyone else was doing it too, Meg reaching for the higher graffiti, Scar with his skirt tucked into his jeans so he could crouch down and do the low parts. They scrubbed it out. The hatred that shone clearly in daylight was disappearing. When it was done, Brew walked over to Sara and held out his can. I thought it was over, that somehow Sara was collecting the cans and then we'd leave. But she gave her can to Brew and they both returned to their spots. Brew wrote so quickly that I guessed he must have known what he wanted to write in advance. He stood and stretched and crouched to make the letters long and wide, filling in the blank space with yellow words.

THIS PLASE IS EVRYONE'S

A message to the original offenders. A warning.

I glanced around to watch Meg and Scar and Sara and Seany writing their own messages:

YOU MATTER
DON'T LISTEN TO BIGOTS
BE BETTER
BE YOURSELF

No. Not a message for the sectarian bozos. A message for the kids in the park.

They were halfway through replacing the hateful graffiti when I heard a shout and then Brew in my ear telling me to run, grabbing my hand but not in the way I thought that he might, and pulling me out of the park. The six of us made off into the night, the light of a single police torch behind us, but only for a while. Still, we kept on running until we got back to the courts. The rain was lightly blowing in our faces and I felt I could have run for miles with Brew still holding my hand even when it was clear that we'd lost the cop. I wondered if the rest of them felt this way as well. Full of power and possibility. I wondered how many times they'd been chased by the police.

When I finally flopped onto a floor cushion I realised how sore my legs were. I felt so heavy and at the same time so full of light that I just wanted to laugh and laugh. The little group hugged one another, laughing at the success of their 'mission' and I watched them from my spot on the floor. They looked like a family congratulating someone for passing a hard exam, only it was everyone who had passed the exam. Meg stood in front of me and held both hands out.

'Come! Come, Tilly! Celebrate with us!'

I took her hands and let her help me to my feet and she scooped me into her arms.

'Well *done*!' She beamed. She smelled of expensive perfume and her hair was still immaculate in its bob. Everyone else looked bedraggled and Seany had paint all over his hands, but Meg looked as though she'd just stepped off a film set. She slipped off her trainers and into a pair of silver heels.

'Right then!' she announced, clapping her hands. 'This calls for a little drink, lovelies!'

A cheer went up and Meg and Brew left the room as everyone else sat down on the cushions. I was glad to be sitting again. I looked at my phone. 1.30 a.m. No later than one of my usual climbs, but I wondered if I should be getting back. So far nothing had gone wrong, but it could have. I shivered, thinking of how Dad's face would have looked if he'd been woken by that cop bringing me home and telling him what I'd been up to. I knew it could never happen again, yet even as I said it to myself I knew that it would. I knew it because of Scar's kind eyes as he sat beside me, grinning. I knew it because of him and Seany high fiving and giggling like little kids. I knew it because of Meg and her reassuring hug. I knew it because they'd done something good. Really good. They hadn't had time to replace all of the horrible messages, but they'd done enough. And I'd been there. Almost part of it. And I knew it because I knew that I needed to see Brew again. I wanted to be in the gang.

Brew and Meg returned, both of them carrying beer bottles of different shapes and sizes. They handed them round. I took one, looking up at Brew.

'Don't worry,' he said. 'It's just beer – my own brew. You drink? If not we have some Coke somewhere . . . '

'No, it's OK.' I took the bottle. 'I'd like to try your beer.'

It was my first beer. I'm not against alcohol but it just never appealed to me – going down the docks, drinking cheap cider from massive bottles like the kids from school at weekends. This was different, but I didn't want Dad to know that I'd been out drinking so I'd just have one.

It was cold and fizzy and bitter, and I liked it. I wiped my mouth.

'You like it?' asked Brew, taking a long pull from his own bottle.

'I do!'

'Heh. Don't sound so surprised. It's good stuff!'

'It's cold.'

'Yeah, you got a cold one. Only two in the cool bag. Meg got the other for doing the ground work tonight.' He grinned over at Meg, who raised her bottle, her perfectly painted nails tapping off the glass.

'Ohhhh, favouritism!' said Scar. 'Some anarchist you are!' He winked at Brew and everyone laughed. Brew smiled and threw a cushion at Scar. And that was how the night continued. They teased each other, drank beer, told stupid stories; Meg even sang a song and after she finished we all clapped and whistled. I thought about the people in my class at school. I felt so far from them and I knew I could never explain anything like this, even if I wanted to. It was a bit like being at the top when I'd done one my climbs. There was space to just 'be'. It was comfortable and it felt free, but I wasn't alone.

I didn't have only one beer. I had two, and then I had some lemonade. Nobody laughed or called me a wuss. In fact, nobody said anything about it. It seemed like the main reason to be there was to be together, and that was all. If you wanted beer, you had beer. If you wanted lemonade, you had lemonade. And at some point during the silliness and the jokes and Meg singing, Brew put his head on my shoulder and I tipped mine slightly so that my cheek was in his dark hair, and that was all – no other contact and nothing said – and when I said I should probably go, he walked me home and kissed the side of my face. He said that he hoped I'd had a good night and that I should think about coming back, but only if I wanted to. I nodded and said that I would, but the truth was that that kiss was burning my skin and it was all I could consider, even after everything, and I knew that the next day I'd remember everything else as well, but for now I would go to bed, trying not to make a sound, pressing my hand to my face, wondering how to blow out a flame from a struck match that I never wanted to burn away.

# Chapter 13

'I knew it might be an issue but, honestly, not *that* much of an issue, but she's just being such a twat about it!'

Beth was stabbing at a piece of rubbery pasta with no real intention of eating it. I chewed my sandwich. The school cafeteria was quiet because it was sunny out and lunch time was almost over. I'd been listening to Beth going on about Daniel and their disastrous date for twenty minutes already and she was showing no signs of stopping for breath.

'I mean, for God's sake, it's 2017. The Troubles were over before I was even born. I knew my parents were bigots but you'd think they wouldn't mind me going out with a Catholic. He's a straight A student and excellent at tennis and they *love* tennis! Like, what is the actual problem with them? Is your dad like that? Does he freak out about religion?'

'I don't really know. I mean, I've never gone out with a Catholic.'

'Except for Shauneen Jackson.' She winked at me.

'One: I did not go out with Shauneen Jackson. It was just a kiss. Two: her dad's a Prod.'

'She goes to Mass sometimes, though.'

'Three: you really think my dad's issue with me seeing Shauneen Jackson would be with her religion?'

Beth raised an eyebrow.

'Is your dad a 'phobe? I thought, you know, since he was a journalist he'd be cool with that?'

'What's being a journo got to do with it? He's not a bigot really . . . he's just – old fashioned, I suppose.'

'Like that time he said he thought Nelson Mandela should never have got out of prison?'

'I know . . . but he's not bad really. He kind of finds it hard to imagine that someone else's life might be different to his . . . But sure, you know what paper he works for. They're full of crap about all sorts of stuff.'

'So . . . do you *want* to go out with Shauneen?'

'What? No! For the last time – it was just a kiss!'

'A pretty good kiss though, eh?' Beth nudged me playfully, beaming. I was glad she'd changed the subject from Dreary Daniel and his amazing tennis skills and their ill-fated Romeo and Juliet love affair, but I wasn't interested in Shauneen Jackson. Incredibly soft lips or not, it wasn't her I was thinking about.

'It was a good kiss. But it's in the past. It's kisstory.'

'Kisstory! Hahahaha!'

I put my hand to my cheek, trying to remember Brew's mouth against my skin, just for a second.

'What are you smirking about?' Beth said. 'Hey – is it that guy? Oh my God, I can't believe I forgot to ask you about him! Did he call you? Did you meet him? Tell me!'

The bell rang. I grinned and pushed my chair under the table. I did want to tell her but it would have to wait.

'Eeek! Just give me a quick summary!' she shrieked, grabbing my arm. 'On the way to English! Just the main details: kiss or no kiss?' We walked out of the canteen, arm in arm.

'Kiss.'

'Arghhh!' She did a little jump in the air. 'On the lips? Tongue?'

'Urgh. Peck on the check. Tiny amount of hand-holding. No big deal.'

Past the lockers and the groups of kids hanging on to their last moments of lounging about.

'No big deal?!' she said, way too loudly.

'SSSSSHHHHH!' I giggled.

'It is a big deal, though!'

'Why? I hardly know him.'

'Because you know as well as I do, he is *hot*!'

I laughed out loud and Mrs Matchett rolled her eyes. A line of first years filed neatly into her room, their big eyes watching us sharing our secrets and trying not to burst out laughing.

'Seriously though,' said Beth as we rounded the corner, 'is he your boyfriend now?'

'What? No!' Although I hoped he was thinking about it, because I was thinking about it, and it was true that I didn't really know anything about him, but I had spent the rest of the weekend imagining being his girlfriend, imagining who he might be, imagining being part of their happy gang of misfits, putting the wrongs of the world right, and then the two of us heading off on our own into the dark ruins of the courthouse to be together alone. I wondered if he was thinking the same thing.

We got to Mr White's room and he grunted at us – something about being late – and we sat down, Beth giving my hand an excited squeeze before letting me retreat into the world of Shakespeare and poetry and the long story I was writing in my own mind.

If only things were that easy – writing your own story, having everything work out right. But I knew that even if Brew was thinking about me too, there was going to be a major problem in the form of a certain eager and highly protective journalist. What I didn't realise was how soon my problems were going to start.

# Chapter 14

I should have picked it up by the silence. I was sitting upstairs at my desk looking through the same passage of verse over and over, trying to concentrate and make the words go in. I heard the door shut, the footsteps, the kitchen chair scrape over the tiles. But no 'It's me!' or 'I'm home'. I should have known from that.

Fifteen minutes later, knowing that the bloody poet's words weren't going to mean anything at any point that evening, I got up and went downstairs. Dad was sitting at the kitchen table with the open paper in front of him, but he wasn't looking at it. He was staring dead ahead.

'Hi, Dad. You OK?'

He turned his head, slowly, to look at me.

'Just tell me the truth,' he said.

I felt my chest tighten. I wanted to run. Oh shit oh shit. What did he know? The park? The climbing? Everything?

I couldn't answer.

His voice softened and he rubbed his temples with his fingertips.

'Come here. Sit down. I just. I just want to know what's going on.'

I hadn't done anything wrong. Not really. So why did I feel guilty? I sat down opposite him and he pointed to the paper.

'Have a look. Here.' He turned the page around so I could see it.

# Gang Of Unknowns Vandalises Children's Play Park

I wanted to tell him it was a lie. That the group were putting things right, not messing them up. But that wasn't what he was pointing out. There was a photograph. CCTV. It was blurred, but you could make out three figures running away. You could see . . .

'That's you.' He jabbed at the picture, frowning. 'Isn't it? It's you.'

It was me. Nobody else would have known. It was just the back of my head. The back of my coat. My hand reaching out, holding Brew's. Me, running. A policeman behind us. Oh God.

'It's not what you think, Dad.'

He sat back in his chair, shaking his head, looking at the picture.

'I don't even know what to think,' he said quietly. 'You were studying last night. You were working. And then you went to bed. How?' He jabbed the photograph. 'And who on earth are these people?'

The tears were running down my face. How on earth could I explain this? I couldn't. But I knew it was over. I knew that Dad knew it too because he didn't go mad. He didn't shout or swear. It was more serious than that. Eventually he spoke again.

'I was a teenager once myself, you know, Tilly. I did stupid, reckless things too. I can't pretend to understand why a girl like you would vandalise a child's play area, but . . .'

'We didn't!'

I hadn't meant to burst out. It was the wrong thing to do. Dad took a deep breath in. I knew it meant I shouldn't say another word but I had to, I just had to. It wasn't as if things could get any worse anyway.

'They weren't writing graffiti, they were rubbing it out! Writing positive things, good things!'

'Well, they either wrote things on the wall or they didn't.'

'They did – not all of it – just the good things. You should have seen what it was like before!'

'So their vandalism wasn't as bad as someone else's, is that what you're saying?'

'*No!* I mean, yes. I mean . . . they're not a gang. Not like that!'

'Oh?' He folded his arms. His mouth was grim. I knew he was boiling inside. 'And what are they like, Tilly? Who exactly are they?'

I could hear next door's telly on. The hall clock ticking. The hum of the dishwasher.

'Well, that shut you up, didn't it?' he said. 'I'll tell you what, Tilly, and this is a One Time Only offer. You will never see those people again. Do you understand?'

I nodded, looking at the tabletop, which was getting splashed with tears.

'And in return,' he went on, 'I will not ask you about those people. OK? I won't ask their names and I won't tell the police that my good, innocent, grammar school daughter has gotten herself mixed up with them. Understand?'

I nodded again.

He stood up and straightened out his shirt.

'But you mark my words, young lady. If I get so much as a tiny hint that you are going around with this group of yobbos again, you will be accompanying me to the local police station without hesitation.'

I looked up at him. Would he really do that? Tout on his own kid just to get a load of people he didn't know in trouble? He raised his eyebrows as if to say *yes, I am serious*, and I believed him. It wasn't just about the 'vandalism', it was about me. He needed me to be that 'good, innocent, grammar school daughter', because if I wasn't then what was he? The dad of a vandal? A failed parent? He meant it all right.

That's what Dad is like. He was always telling me, 'Say what you mean, and mean what you say, Tilly,' and that's what he did. He never lost his head, even when I ran away with Davy Jordan when we were eleven. We had planned to spend the night in the hut we'd made in the park out of wood they'd collected for the bonfires, but it wasn't as much fun as we'd thought and in the middle of the night some bigger kids came and threatened to chuck us on the fire if we didn't piss off and leave their gear alone. We were so scared that we ran home in the dark, both of us crying. My dad hugged me, put me to bed, and in the morning he said, 'Tilly, you're grounded. For a month.' A month! That was almost the whole summer. But it was exactly four weeks before he let me out to play with Davy Jordan again. There was no point arguing with Dad once he'd made his mind up about something.

I stood up and did my best to keep my voice from breaking. 'Thanks, Dad. And I'm sorry.'

He smiled a serious smile, and that was that. Everything had broken. I went to my room, turned out the light, lay down on my bed and cried. I didn't go down for dinner and Dad didn't call me. I suppose he knew that we both needed some space. I didn't even feel like going for a climb. I just wanted not to move, not to 'be' anywhere. I drifted into my story, trying to imagine that it hadn't been real. After all, I didn't really know them. Maybe it wasn't OK to do graffiti, even if it was good graffiti. Maybe they had done worse things, who knows? Sean had nicked my bike. Maybe they all nicked stuff? But the more I tried to convince myself, the more I saw Scar's friendly, open face. Meg, passing round drinks, making sure everyone was OK. Brew, with his head on my shoulder. I tortured myself into a deep sleep and I had no idea what time it was when my phone text alert buzzed in my ear, jolting me awake.

# Chapter 15

'So, Daniel thinks that his mum can talk to my mum at the tennis club and smooth everything over. She's *so* nice, his mum. Apparently she got hassle when she was a kid for dating a Protestant. You'd think that would make her really angry, wouldn't you? But she's not. She's lovely, and I think she really likes me, and . . . are you even listening to this?'

I wasn't. I was miles away. Letting her drivel on about Mr Perfect But Boring as I counted the tiles on the canteen counter across the room. I kept getting lost around six and going back to the start.

'Sorry,' I said. I tried to smile at Beth but I couldn't manage it really.

'Oh my God, Tills, what's wrong? You look like shit.'

'Thanks.'

She caught my grin and smiled back.

'That's better. Is it Brew? Did he try it on?'

'What? No!'

I picked up my limp sandwich and put it back down again.
I might as well tell her. It was over now anyway. Brew hadn't
texted me since the party until the night that Dad found out.
Nice timing. The first text had been brief, suggesting another
meetup for coffee. I had deleted it and deleted his number. But
then he texted again an hour later 'just in case the first hadn't
sent properly'. I'd thought about telling him to stay away but I
couldn't bring myself to type it, so I just deleted that text too.
A final text at 11 a.m. this morning.:

*I don't stalk girls. If you don't want to hang out again it's fine.
This is my last text. Bye Tilly. You were the coolest.*

That one, I kept. Nobody had ever called me cool before.
I wanted so much to text him back. No. I wanted to get my
trainers on, get on my bike and go back to the courthouse.
And it wasn't just him. I wanted to be with them all again. But
I couldn't risk it. Dad wasn't kidding – he'd be keeping such
a close eye on me and if I went back he'd find them sooner
or later, and maybe he'd tell the police about them. I took a
breath and began to tell Beth.

'Did you see that thing in the paper last night? The one
about . . . '

'Oh my God, yes! About Brad Pitt!'

'No, flip sake, not Brad Pitt. About the park.'

'Um . . . not sure?'

'Well, there's this gang. Of "unknowns". They did some
graffiti . . . '

'Oh, I *did* hear about that. Dad was going on about it
because it's the park he used to take us to. Some sectarian graffiti or something? Dicks. What about it?'

I took a drink of water to give myself time to think about what exactly to say. Should I tell her the whole thing? About climbing? No. Small bits of information. I could trust her, I thought. And it was all over now anyway.

'Brew was in the gang.'

Her mouth fell open and I took a bite of the tuna and onion sandwich. It was damp but I'd been too miserable to eat breakfast and I was starving. It tasted good. I had half the sandwich eaten before she spoke.

'But, he seemed so nice!'

'He is nice.'

'But, you just said . . .'

'Look.' I set down the sandwich crusts and looked Beth in the eyes. 'You can't tell anyone this. Not even Daniel. OK?'

'OK, I swear!' She was dying for the information, but I knew Beth. She was my best friend in the world and always had been. She wouldn't tell.

'It's not how the papers have reported it. They weren't writing horrible stuff. They painted over the sectarian stuff and wrote other messages.'

'What other messages?'

'Nice things. Messages to the little kids. Things like: you are fine just as you are.'

Beth's eyes widened.

'That's *so* lovely! Oh my God, Tilly! Why did the paper say they'd written the bad stuff?'

'I don't even think they read the messages. They just knew it was graffiti, which is technically against the law, so they are criminals, really . . .' I shrugged. 'Anyway, Dad saw the CCTV pic and he knew it was me even though my back was turned to the camera. So that's the end of that . . . '

'You were there?! Oh *no!*'

'Ssssh!' A couple of kids at the table next to us had looked over, obviously wondering what had made Beth so animated. 'Keep it down.'

'Sorry,' she whispered, leaning in. 'Oh my God, Tilly! Can't you tell your dad what the craic is? Surely he could see that they, I mean, you, were doing something nice?'

'Have you met my dad?'

That shut her up. Everyone knew Dad. Everyone knew the paper he wrote for and the kind of articles they printed. People's parents used to joke that they'd have to tone down their arguments when I was round at a friend's house in case they read about it in the paper the next day. You can't talk my dad out of a story that he's made his mind up about. You might as well try to change the colour of the sky.

The bell rang. The dinner ladies started giving people glances and wiping empty tables.

'What are you going to do?' Beth asked.

I shrugged. In reality, I was going to go to class, go home, do my homework, have my dinner, watch TV and go to bed. And during all of that I'd read Brew's text about fifty times. *You were the coolest.* Eventually I'd delete it and then maybe eventually I'd forget about it and that would be that. But one look at Beth told me it wasn't going to be an option.

I shook my head.

'Whatever it is you're thinking, Beth, forget it. It's over. I'm not risking anything with my dad. He's a proper hard arse.'

She was grinning.

'I'll think of something.'

'Seriously, Beth. No, you won't.'

She linked arms with me and led me out of the lunch room.

'Yes I will. I always do.'

# Chapter 16

It's funny how telling someone a secret can make you feel safe and unsafe all at the same time. I knew Beth wouldn't tell anyone, but all the same – it was out there now. If my dad was the torturing type – and I wasn't completely sure that he wasn't – he could find out that I was still thinking of Brew, because now there was someone to find out from. But as I went to sleep that night there was a tiny flicker of warmth in my chest that soothed me. I wasn't alone. And even though I knew that with every moment that passed Brew was slipping away and forgetting me, there was still a thought – a tiny, tiny hope – that maybe Beth was right and she'd somehow find a way. I knew it was crazy, because how could she? If I couldn't think of a way to keep on seeing Brew and the rest of the group then I didn't see how she could come up with anything. It wasn't as if she was winning any awards for Rebel of the Year. But at least I wasn't alone with the thought. It was enough to get me at least one night's sleep, anyway.

I didn't have too long to wait. The phone ringing woke me

up. I heard Dad answering: 'Yes, please do come over. Give her half an hour – you know what she's like before she's had a cup of tea.' Dad was always delighted to have Beth over. If only he knew that she wasn't coming round to discuss whether or not Ophelia in *Hamlet* was a feminist.

Half an hour later on the dot Beth was sitting in my room, make-up perfect, hair immaculate, shiny and black, clipped back with a red flower pin. She sat at the top of the bed, back against the wall, balancing neon pink heels on the chest of drawers. I sat on the opposite end of the bed, still in my Muppet pyjamas, hair scraped back in a ponytail, sipping my third cup of strong tea.

'You sure you don't want some?'

'No. Caffeine first thing in the morning is terrible for your skin,' she said.

'Lack of caffeine's terrible for my murderous tendencies.'

She grinned, filing her turquoise nails.

'I'm really not sure about this colour,' she said.

'Well, don't look at me. I can't even see colours until tea number five.'

I pulled the duvet round me. How could someone so perfect have such terrible dress sense? I imagined her when we were older. I'd probably have a boring job in some law firm, filing things, while Beth would be employing personal shoppers and stylists to hide the fact that, left to her own devices, she'd be dressed like Coco the clown on a daily basis. But she didn't want to talk about the future, or her nails.

'So,' she said, turning to face me. She folded her legs in a criss-cross. 'Have you still got Brew's number?'

'Sssssh! Keep it down. And no, I deleted it.'

'Argh! Idiot!'

I rolled my eyes. But, hang on. I grabbed my phone. Sure enough – his last text. I'd kept it. Reading it again made me wince but I still had it – his number.

'Let's see it?' said Beth, reaching out for the phone.

'No way!' I pulled it back, almost spilling the tea. 'Not until I know exactly what you're going to do with it.'

'OK, well, duh, *obviously* I'm going to call him.'

'Huh. No you are not.'

'Why not? You can't see him again if you don't talk to him.'

'It's really nothing to do with him, though, is it? It's Dad that's the big problem.'

She pursed her lips as if I was being a naughty little girl who didn't want her help.

'Go and get dressed and let's go into town. I need new nail polish, and we can chat on the way. Who knows,' she said, eyes twinkling, 'Mr Sexy might be busking again!'

I made a 'puke' gesture and headed for the bathroom, taking the phone with me.

# Chapter 17

'Town's busy today,' said Beth, peering through the bus window.

As the bus approached the stop outside City Hall you could see there were more people around than usual. It wasn't raining, for once, and Belfast was always busy on a Saturday but as we drew closer to the stop you could see something else – a gathering. Maybe about a hundred people crowded round the City Hall, some with placards. Not a huge event, but enough to draw the attention of shoppers who stood a few feet away looking on, just far enough so you knew they weren't part of the protest, but they were interested.

'What's on today?' I asked the bus driver, nodding towards the crowd.

He frowned.

'Nothing you'd want to know about, love,' he said. Beth gave me a *look* and we got off the bus and headed to the corner to see what the fuss was all about.

There was a man standing on a bench outside the fence

which surrounds the City Hall. He had a microphone and a tiny amplifier which made his voice distorted but I could make out some of the words it hissed out across the crowd: *immigrants. Economy. Local. Benefits.*

The man was shouting and waving a piece of paper in his other hand and every so often the crowd would cheer and wave their pieces of paper.

'I don't like this,' said Beth.

I didn't like it either. The onlookers were shaking their heads and gripping their kids, but the man was still ranting on and the people cheering got louder.

'I'm going to get a better look,' I said.

'Oh my God – do not!' said Beth.

'It's OK, I'll be careful. You stay here.'

I could hear her telling me to wise up as I moved closer to the crowd. I just wanted to find out who they were. There had been protests in town before – sometimes against government cuts, sometimes protests calling for peace after a riot. But I hadn't seen anything like this before. Everyone there was dressed in black. From a distance they looked like a black cloud gathered at the entrance to the city.

I hung back far enough so that I didn't stick out in my blue hoody, but I could see them more clearly now. Mostly men, hardly any women. Lots of them had their hoods up even though the weather was good. I could see a placard which read **LOCAL HOMES FOR LOCAL PEOPLE**. On the ground in front of me someone had dropped one of the pieces of paper. I picked it up.

**IT'S TIME TO ASK WHY!**
**WHY? Why can't local people get housing when**
**foreigners are living in our social housing?**
**WHY? Why can't local people get benefits when**
**immigrants are living off the state?**
**WHY? Why should we put up with this?**
**CHARITY BEGINS AT HOME!**

I wanted to drop it again but I didn't want to draw attention to myself. I wanted to get as far away from them as I could. The speaker was getting more animated and now someone else had joined him on the bench and between the two of them they were holding up a Union Jack flag. A flag I'd seen all my life. I knew that some people didn't like it – some people preferred the flag of the Irish Republic – but for me the Union Jack seemed OK and normal. But now in the hands of those angry men it felt different. Their faces were hard and their mouths were wide and I knew that I didn't belong there, standing with them. And so I turned to leave but just as I did I caught something out of the corner of my eye and I turned back.

It happened quickly. A smaller person, also dressed in black and holding a flyer, had come out of the crowd and jumped onto the bench and he was wrenching the flag from the hands of the two men. One of the men lost his balance and stumbled back, dropping the flag as he reached for the back of the bench. The intruder threw the flag to the ground and then ripped up the flyer, shouting 'FUCK THE FASCISTS!' He thrust a fist above his head, hopped up onto the back of the seat and launched himself over the fence surrounding City Hall.

It took a few seconds for the men on the bench and their supporters in the front row to figure out what had happened and push through the City Hall gates, but by that time the figure was running away, trailing the flag behind him. The crowd were starting to shout and the police began to move in. I ran back to Beth, who had tears in her eyes.

'You idiot!' she said. 'You could've . . . '

'Did you see him?'

I was breathless, pulling Beth away from the scene, but I could've run a mile.

'Did you see who it was?' I asked her.

'No. Who? That kid who took the flag? What a total IDIOT!'

'Hero, more like. Did you see him?'

'Yeah, I just said. Stop pulling me.'

She wriggled out of my grip and we stopped. I took her arm.

'It was Brew, Beth. It was him. I saw his face. He took the flag.'

I knew I was grinning like a crazy person but I couldn't help it. Nothing was solved. But something had changed. It had been a crazy thing to do – Beth was right. He could've been beaten to a pulp by those gorillas. But he wasn't. He got away. He showed them up as the racist twats they were and he got away. And watching it filled me with a nerve that I never knew I had, as if all of his bravery had spread out to touch every person who felt the same. Screw it. I had to see him again. I had to be part of this group of crazy, brave, amazing people. You're only young once, right? And I wasn't going to get old and be one of those onlookers, shaking my head and clutching my kids but doing nothing.

Beth was giving me the same look she'd given me on the bus earlier.

'Are you all right?' she said, 'You look, I dunno, a bit crazed or something.'

I took her arm and led her towards the shops.

'Come on, Beth. Let's sort out your nail polish before the fashion cops arrest you and you can buy me a coffee and we'll make the plot to end all plots!'

'I think I'm changing my mind about Brew, Tilly . . .'

'Me too.'

# Chapter 18

I was on the phone to Brew before Beth could say anything else. When he picked up he was breathless.

'Hi, Tilly. I wasn't expecting to hear from—'

'I saw it! I saw you! Oh my *God*, Brew. That was amazing!'

Beth looked worried and I turned slightly so I couldn't see her face.

'Heh!' He was still breathing hard and it occurred to me that maybe he was still running.

'Are you somewhere safe?' I said.

'Nearly! I'll call you back when I get there.'

'OK. Jesus. Sorry for calling. I just . . .'

'Nah, it's grand. I'm glad you did! Speak to you in a bit!'

He hung up. I turned back to Beth. She was standing with her arms folded. She didn't say anything but I knew that she was thinking that I was mad. That Brew was mad. She was crossing over – starting to side with Dad. Oh God, what if she really did start to side with him? She might tell him!

'We need to talk,' I said.

'Yuh think?' She smiled a half smile.

'Let's go to Boots first and check out the make-up,' I suggested.

It would give me a chance to stop buzzing and come back down to earth. But as we went into the store all I could think about was him, and it wasn't just him and those amazing eyes. It was all of them and how bold they were. Beth was picking out lipsticks, rubbing the testers on the heel of her hand, checking the colours one against the other. I pretended to look at the various shades of sparkly eyeliner but all I could think about was how I didn't even have the guts to wear this stuff and they were living completely fearless lives and I wanted to be like them but it was so far from my life – so far from me. A few hours ago I'd been ready to jack them all in, to never see Brew again, or Meg, or Scar. After one of the best nights of my life I'd been ready to give up the chance of ever doing it again just because I couldn't defy my dad. They could stand up to racist dickheads who probably would've kicked their heads in without hesitation, and I couldn't risk even a little lie to my dad. Pathetic! But now I had a chance – a chance to be like them. A chance to be *with* them.

'OK, I'm done,' said Beth, both hands full with lipsticks, eyeshadows, nail polish. 'You getting anything?'

I looked at the glittery eyeliner.

'Actually, yeah,' I said, choosing the blue one.

We walked to the till together. As Beth was paying my phone buzzed against my hip. I wanted to answer it but it wasn't the right time. Before I spoke to Brew I needed to work on Beth and bring her completely over to my side again. I'd text and explain. I took my phone out of my pocket but it hadn't been Brew after all. It was a text from Dad.

**Just heard there's been trouble in town. You all right? Keep in touch. Dad. X**

My heart sank. Dad wasn't one of those racist idiots. He was just my dad. He was worried about me. I knew I had to see Brew and the others again but it wasn't going to be easy lying to Dad. I was going to need Beth more than ever. I texted him back. Then I texted Brew.

**Hope you're OK. Call me after 6pm if you can. Tilly.**

I thought about whether or not to put an 'X' on the end of the text. The woman behind the till shouted 'Next!' and I looked at the glittery blue eyeliner in my hand. I added the 'X', clicked 'send' and walked to the till.

# Chapter 19

As Beth and I walked home we laughed and chatted about videos we'd seen on YouTube and Facebook. Stupid stuff. We had exhausted all the serious talk by then. It was sunny and we were full of sugar and silliness and our pockets were empty.

Beth hadn't been so hard to persuade. She could see that what Brew had done was heroic. She just thought it was too risky, and she was worried about me getting 'caught up with it all'. We had sat in Delaney's for an hour and a half discussing only one topic.

'I won't do anything stupid,' I had said, sipping my milk-shake. 'I have to keep a low profile anyway, because of Dad.'

'Well, OK ...' she said, her forehead wrinkled. 'You'll let me know, if anything happens. Anything bad. If you're in trouble, I mean?'

'Yeah, of course!'

And I meant it. I told Beth everything then – all about the group, my bike, the squat in the old courts. The only thing I left out was the climbing. That was still mine. It was enough that Brew knew about it. I still needed a way to be truly on my own. So I didn't tell her about that, even though it felt a bit sneaky somehow. But a person has a right to some privacy, don't they? Maybe I'd tell her later. Just not yet.

'So,' said Beth after I'd told her everything I knew, 'you're in with this . . . gang?'

'I suppose so,' I said. 'I mean, they're really friendly, but it's not like they asked me to join or anything. But I think they'd be cool with it if I showed up again.'

'And . . . are they cool if *anyone* shows up?'

Uh-oh. I could tell where this was going.

'To be honest, Beth, I don't know. I really don't know a lot about how it works. I mean, I could ask?'

'Well . . . ' She was playing it cool, relaxed in the coffee shop sofa with her legs crossed, sipping her shake. But I wondered if she was feeling a tiny bit left out. If I'd been her I probably would have. 'It's fine either way,' she continued, 'but I'd love to meet Mr Brew.' She gave me a wink.

'You make him sound like Mr Grey, from *50 Shades*.'

She spluttered milkshake.

'Hahahaha! Is *that* why you like him so much?' She laughed, adopting a deep husky voice. 'Does he call you Anastasia?'

'Ssssh!' People were looking over at us carrying on. 'We'll get kicked out for arsing about.'

'Haha! Well, you never know, Tills. He could be big into all that stuff. Handcuffs. Whips . . . '

'Sssssshhhh!' I laughed.

I had to admit, though, she was right that I hardly knew Brew. I mean, it wasn't like I hadn't wondered about what it would be like to kiss him properly. But I hadn't thought about what if he was a proper weirdo or anything.

Beth gave me an exaggerated wink and we both cracked up. The elderly man at the table next to us tutted. His wife grinned at us when he wasn't looking. We were down to the dregs of our drinks and Beth started putting her phone into her bag.

'Is Brew a Prod, then?'

It was a question I wasn't expecting.

'I don't know.'

'What's his real name?'

'I don't know.'

Beth went quiet and I knew what that meant. She was worrying. Or judging me. Or both, probably. But she was right. It suddenly struck me that I had met Brew outside any normal situation. Not at a youth group. Not in school. Not even in the park.

The waitress was starting to put chairs up on the empty tables and Beth began to gather her things.

Not that Brew's religion would have mattered to me in the slightest. Even Dad wouldn't have cared about that sort of thing – it wasn't like we were religious ourselves. But it was a starting point. If you know someone's name or school or where they live, you can have a pretty good guess at their religion. Catholics go to Catholic schools, Protestants go to state schools. The only tricksy ones are the integrated schools – you don't know who you're talking to then. But you could still guess by the area they live in. And if you know their religion you can guess at other things too. You might be wrong but it's still a start. You could guess what sports they might be into, what kind of music or dancing they might have learnt in school.

I had nothing to go on – no starting point. Facts I knew about Brew:

He was gorgeous.

He knew how to make beer.

He was pretty chilled out.

He was brave.

I wanted to see him again as soon as possible.

And that was it. How could I be so into someone I knew so little about? What age was he? Maybe he was one of those blokes who looks like they're a teenager when actually they're in their thirties? Shit. Maybe he was actually married or something. Or a proper criminal. I wondered if he'd been in jail. Maybe anything!

We were the last to leave the cafe and our waitress saluted us and locked the door behind us. I made up my mind to find out as much as I could as soon as possible. I checked my phone: 5.25 p.m. Not long until I heard from him again.

It was 6.15 p.m. by the time we got back to my place. We were in my room, sitting on the bed, and Brew texted at 6.30 p.m. I felt my phone vibrate and I took a breath before looking at it.

**Party tomorrow night at our place. It'll totally kill. Hope you can come. B x**

I caught my breath at the 'x' on his signature. Did it mean what I wanted it to mean? The thought of it made me remember GCSE maths:

**Find the value of 'X' in this equation.**

X = 'I like you'?

X = 'I wish this was a real kiss'?

'Loverboy?' asked Beth.

I nodded.

'Well?'

'Wait a sec.'

I texted Brew back:

**Can I bring my friend Beth? She'll not say anything.**

The phone vibrated again almost as soon as it had sent.

**Yeah. NP. If you trust her.**

I did trust her. Beth had been my best friend for ever. She was still the only person who knew that I'd nicked pick 'n' mix from the cinema that time, and she never once told anyone about the time when I drank three shots of peach schnapps and threw up in her parents' bathroom. She was silly and sometimes a bit naive but she was definitely loyal.

'Beth, do you think your folks will let you stay at mine tomorrow night?'

'Hmmm.' She frowned. 'Dunno. School the next morning.'

Damn.

'But!' She smiled again. 'I *am* free first double on Mondays. So I could promise to get to my first class on time. I've been really good this term ... They might go for it ... Why?'

I grinned.

'We're going to a party. It's going to be amazing. And if my dad finds out, he's going to ground me for the rest of my life.'

# Violent Teen Disrupts Peaceful Gathering at City Hall

# Chapter 20

I didn't lie to Dad. Not exactly. I told him we were going to a party and that we both had a double free in the morning and that I was going with Beth. All true. Obviously I didn't mention whose party it was, or where it was happening, and I didn't mention the riot that was going on outside it, but to be fair I had no idea that was going to happen myself.

I texted Brew from the corner.

Er. I can't get anywhere near the place. Dickheads throwing bricks at the cops everywhere.

He replied quickly.

Shit, yeah, I forgot to tell you. Come round the back way on Florence Place. Shouldn't be a problem.

I have to admit, I wasn't too excited about taking a route I didn't completely know, not when the air was so tense with violence already. Beth was clearly rattled as well.

'God, maybe this isn't such a great idea, Tilly. DVD and a pizza sounds like a plan right now ...'

'Come on,' I said, leading her down the other street. 'We'll give this a go and if it doesn't work out we'll go home for that pizza and call it a day.'

The street was black and quiet as we turned into it but that was a good sign. No cop cars flashing their blue lights, nobody singing songs about torturing hunger strikers. From what I could tell there wasn't even any glass on the ground. We could hear the rattle of the riot continuing but it was dying out as we walked further from the main road. As my eyes adjusted to the darkness I could make out the back of the courthouse. Yes, that was definitely it. I could tell by the silhouette of the roof that I had scaled just a few days ago. There was a light on. I took Beth's arm and we led each other towards it.

'You ready?' I said.

'Yeah!' she said. 'I'm just glad to be off the road.'

Brew was at the window waiting for us and carrying a large candle. He grinned and gave me a hug. He smelt of fresh tobacco and men's shower gel. I wondered where he managed to shower. I introduced Beth and he hugged her too.

'Come on in, then!' He went before us into the dark building and led us to a different room to the one I'd been in the other night. As we approached it the music grew louder, a pulsing electronic rhythm with heavy bass. 'Welcome to Belfast' he said, opening the double doors.

Beth couldn't stop her mouth falling open and I have to admit, although I'd been impressed by the room I'd been in the time before, this was something else.

It was a courtroom. An old, wrecked, dusty courtroom. There were rows of tiered benches with little doors on the end, like in a church, only they were facing the dock, not the altar. Some of the seats were bashed up but most were OK and people were sitting everywhere, laughing on the backs of the benches, facing one another on the floor, drinking out of mugs which were stacked up on a table near the front. The dock had a DJ, his head dipping in time to the bass, one hand on his headphone, one hand on the deck. There was a massive piece of cardboard in front of the dock. It had a painting of a skeleton dressed in a headscarf and covered with flowers.

'Come on in!' said Brew, bouncing in time to the beat. 'I'll get you a drink. You can have anything as long as it's beer.'

'Two beers please!' giggled Beth, clearly mesmerised by the whole thing.

As Brew ducked off to get the drinks she grabbed my arm.

'Oh my *God*, Tills – *look* at this place!'

Above us hung the charred bones of what were once massive light fittings hung to a panelled ceiling shedding dried paint. A couple of people were dancing with their drinks raised above their heads at the front of the room. There were more paintings on the sides of the room – all done on these giant boards – more skeletons, some dancing, some embracing, all decorated with bright flowers and spirals. It was like heaven and hell all at once.

'Well? What do you think?' said Brew, returning with the drinks. He was grinning so wide I wondered if he'd taken something more than just his beer. But he seemed OK so far. *Maybe this is what joy looks like, Tilly. Lighten up . . .*

'It's amazing!' Beth said. 'But – how did you do all this? There's electricity? I thought this place was a ruin?'

'It is!' Brew took a drink from his cup. 'We have some electricity. Meg sorted us with a generator but we only use it when we need to. And running water too! She sorted that out as well. Some rooms are safer than others, but it scrubs up OK, doesn't it?'

'It really does,' I said, gazing at the colourful walls. There was so much to look at. 'What's with all the Halloween decorations?'

'You like them? I painted Santa Muerte there, on the dock.'

'Who?'

'Santa Muerte!' he said, louder. 'She's the Mexican saint of the dead. Here—' He handed me a mug with beer in it. It was freezing. We found an empty pew and opened the little door to go inside. Beth and I sat on the back of the pew, our feet on the seat, while Brew balanced on the back of the one in front, facing us.

'I like the music,' I said. It was hard to keep still, the beat was so steady, it was like when the doctor hits your knee with a little hammer and you can't help jerking out your leg. Beth's foot was tapping on the seat of the pew and I could feel myself swaying in time as well.

'You haven't seen anything yet,' said Brew.

'More to come, then?'

'Oh yes.' He raised his mug and I chinked it with my own.

'You're not worried about the cops hearing all this? They're practically outside the door.'

'Nah. That's why we had the party tonight. Riot nights are

always the best ones. Every cop in town is occupied. They can't hear a thing through the bricks and petrol bombs, and how many of them do you think would suspect a bunch of people having a session right under their noses? All we have to do is make sure that we end our party before themmuns out there end theirs. And they're total party animals.'

I could feel my shoulders relax as the beer buzz spread out over my body. The red and yellow and turquoise paintings made the room feel warmer than it possibly could have been, even with all these people in it. It did feel safe. How weird was that. Safe, in a squat full of strangers in a room covered with skeletons. But I could tell that Beth was feeling it too because she was looking around and smiling and then she said, 'Well, I'm sure you two have a lot of talking to do, so I'm going to have a walk around and look at this death saint of yours.'

She patted my knee on her way past and she left the pew with her mug of beer and went over to look at the walls.

'Don't look like that, she'll be OK,' said Brew. 'Everyone here's like us.'

'What do you mean, "like us"?' I said. And was he including me in the 'us' too, or did he just mean his gang?

'Outsiders,' he said, leaning in towards me and raising both eyebrows. 'Freaks.' He stuck out his tongue, revealing a metal bar studded through it.

He seemed like he was joking but also not really, because looking around he was right – the room was full of the kind of people you never saw on local telly: a guy with a shaved head wearing a vest that showed off two sleeves of tattoos – more skeletons and flowers; a tall girl wearing a stripy beanie and T-shirt to match, and a black miniskirt with ripped leggings that showed her white legs; someone who looked like a woman – high cheekbones, blusher, flowered blouse – and a long plaited beard, and they were talking to another person with a beard, who was wearing a long purple evening dress – but I knew him – it was Scar. I spotted Sara, wearing bright red dungarees and sitting on a table sharing crisps from a large bag with a really tall goth bloke – deathly white face, black lipstick, long black hair, long black woolly jumper, black skinny jeans . . .

Freaks. My dad would call them that too, but he wouldn't mean it the way Brew meant it – as a compliment.

But they weren't frightening. All of them looked happy, even the goth, and they were all moving to the beat as they drank and chatted, and I wished I knew if Brew had meant me as well when he said 'us' but I couldn't ask because I didn't really want to know if he wasn't including me. Because I wasn't like them, really, was I? I might've felt different, inside, but apart from the sparkly blue eyeliner, which now felt a bit pathetic, I was just some kid wearing a hoody and jeans at the coolest party in the whole country.

'Can I have another beer?' I asked.

'Yup, sure.'

He hopped over the pew and I glanced around to see if I could spot Beth again. There she was. She was deep in a conversation with a girl with pink jeans and a purple and yellow tank top. Trust Beth to find the other person in the room who mismatched her clothes. By the time Brew had made his way to the front of the room and back the DJ had stopped and packed up his decks. Scar, in heels which exactly matched his dress, was adjusting a microphone stand to the right of the dock and a guy wearing an Iron Maiden T-shirt in a wheelchair next to him was tuning an acoustic guitar.

'Scar's a singer, then?' I said, as Brew returned.

'Oh wow – wait till you hear him, Tilly!'

And then we stopped talking, and the whole room stopped talking, and every single person had turned to look at Scar and the heavy metal guy, because they were making the most incredible sound. The acoustic guitar wasn't plugged in so the guy was having to beat the strings hard to keep up with Scar's voice, which soared among the burnt remains of the chandeliers. He was singing songs I knew from Disney films when I was a kid but he was making them sound like opera music, or something you'd hear an old-fashioned entertainer singing. With one hand raised and his eyes closed he held the whole congregation so tightly, as if they would've done anything he said. The skeletons on the wall grinned in their static skulls and I imagined the cartoon birds from *Snow White* twittering down to land on Scar's outstretched hand. I didn't know music could be like this.

'Good, isn't he?' said Brew as Scar took several bows to rowdy applause, wolf whistles and stamping.

'Amazing,' I said.

I gripped the back of the pew I was sitting on to steady myself. The music had finished but the feeling it left was hanging in the air like a cloud of electricity. The room was full of noise but I could almost hear my heart thudding in my chest.

'Brew?'

'Aye?'

'I want to know stuff,' I said. 'I want to know everything. I want to know about this place, and about you and everyone in your ... in this group ... Like, I don't even know your real name or anything about, like – like where you live – do you actually live here? Does everyone else? I mean, have you got a job, or ... '

He choked on his beer.

'No, Tilly. I don't have a job.' He held out a hand. 'Come on. I want to show you something.'

I'm not completely thick. I know you don't just feck off with a boy you hardly know at a party in a broken-up squat, leaving your best mate with ... wait, who was Beth with?'

My heart jumped and then settled when my eyes found her, sitting on a table at the front of the room with Sara, both of them swinging their legs and chatting as they leant back against a pile of dusty old books. Beth looked like she was back in the school canteen, chilling with someone she'd known all her life. As we passed them I touched her lightly on the shoulder.

'Oh, hey, Tills!' she said. 'That guy was incredible! And Sara lives right up the road from us. And you see those guys over there?' She pointed to a group of about five large men with bald heads, leather jackets and big boots. 'They're called the Rats! And they make their own motorbikes. How cool is that? They're like the Hell's Angels of Belfast! Did you know we have a Hell's Angels? Mad, isn't it?'

Sara was grinning and I had to admit, Beth's enthusiasm was really sweet. And I could see what she meant. It was mad.

In a good way. It was like this whole other world existed, right in the town that we grew up and got bored in. How could you ever be bored again when you knew about a place like this, about *people* like this?

'Listen, Beth, I'm going off with Brew for a bit.'

She made an 'O' with her mouth and I tried not to feel what she meant but my face was burning.

'We'll be in, erm . . . '

'The tunnel,' said Brew. 'Sara can show you the way if you need us.'

'OK. Enjoy!' sang Beth. She leant over to give me a hug and whispered in my ear, 'Thank you for bringing me to this.' Brew winked at her as he took my hand.

Still full of the energy left by Scar's music, I locked my fingers with his and we left the courtroom together.

# Chapter 21

It was black in the tunnel. And cold. And Brew had let go of my hand.

'Wait a second, Tilly . . . '

For the first time since meeting him I felt slightly afraid and the thought that I'd just put myself in a dangerous position was creeping at the corners of my mind. But Beth knew where I was. Would she hear me if I called? I was still thinking about it when the tunnel suddenly became illuminated and we were standing in a long cave full of colour.

'That's better. Lights are a bit dodgy down here sometimes. You have to kind of jiggle the connection about and one time I was painting right at the end and everything went totally dark and . . . '

'Brew. This is really, like . . . I can't believe this place. Did you do this?'

We were looking down a long hallway with a curved ceiling and, down one whole side, as far as you could see, the walls were painted with a bright mural.

'Yep. All my own work. You wanted to know everything about us, and about me. Well, this is it. Come on.'

He began to walk down the tunnel, turning around to beckon me on.

'Don't look at it! Don't look until we're at the start!'

He sped up and I did too. We were further and further from the doorway and I was further and further from Beth, but I wanted to see it – all of it. I tried not to look but I kept glancing at it. A dog with mad eyes. An old woman crying. Another one of those dancing skeletons. Eventually we reached the end of the tunnel. The beginning. A boy stood looking at us from out of the wall. It was Brew, but younger. No eyeliner. Short, neat haircut. Cute, but sad.

'That's me. Two years ago. When I was fifteen. Except it's not really me, not now.'

Brew turned to me and put his hand on my shoulder and he looked me in the eyes.

'I want you to understand this, Tilly. My name is Brew. That's my real name, because I'm real, and this is me, and I am called Brew. This kid' – he looked at the boy on the wall – 'this is Curtis. He's not very happy, and he's been through some shit. But he got out of it. And he grew up. And he changed his name so that he'll always remember that things have changed for ever and he'll never feel like that again. Do you get it?'

'Yeah.'

I did. I mean, I didn't know exactly what he meant, but I knew I had to not ask about his name again, and that was OK.

'Cool. OK, well . . . '

Brew took his hand from my shoulder and started moving

slowly down the vast mural, telling me the bits of his story he wanted me to hear. I didn't ask him about the crazy-looking woman standing behind the boy with a stick, or about the small pool of what looked like blood beside him. He showed me the boy on a bicycle beside the courthouse. The inside of the dark room where two figures – the boy and someone else – an older woman – were decorating, drawing the big red 'A' that I'd noticed on the wall that first night.

'It's Meg,' he said. 'She was the first one I met.'

'Does she live here too?'

'Haha! Not exactly, no. You've never seen her before?'

'What? No! Why, is she famous or something?'

He shook his head.

'Not really. She doesn't live here – I'm the only one who does.'

The pictures began to show the story of the group. I recognised Scar, looking younger with a shorter beard in sparkly blue leggings and blue high heels. Brew caught me staring at it.

'He used to only dress up for our parties but he dresses like that most of the time now.'

'He's brave.'

'Life's short, Tilly. You have to find yourself and then be yourself. Everyone has to be brave. So anyway,' he continued, 'this is Sara and Seany and me playing together at one of the parties and that's Meg in the corner giving out beer. She was the one who taught me how to make it.'

'You're joking?'

'Nope! She bought me my first kit.'

The comment made me remember something else he'd said.

'Where does . . . I mean, how do you survive here, with no job and stuff? Like, this paint must've cost a fortune?'

It was a bit rude to ask but you have to be brave, right? He didn't seem fazed by it.

'You've seen me busking. I make a bit like that and I have a couple of regular gigs in bars in town. They don't know my age so don't go putting it around that I'm only seventeen, OK?'

'No worries.'

As if I knew anyone who drank in the kind of bars Brew was playing in. I imagined him in a small, dark pub full of old people, not in the cool new nightclubs that the kids in our school went to.

'Meg helps out, though.'

'With money?'

'Yeah.'

'Why does she do that?'

It was all a bit weird, wasn't it? Meg – this older woman who dressed like she was a rich person from old movies – giving cash to young boys and teaching them how to brew beer?

'Don't look like that. She's a good'n, Meg. Seriously. I don't know if I'd even be alive if it wasn't for her. She found this place for me, set me up here, and I know if anyone "normal" knew about her, about what she's done for us here, they'd think she was dead weird, like, but that's why we're hidden, isn't it? If we weren't, we couldn't exist. I couldn't exist. Because it's not normal. I'm not normal.'

'You are!'

We continued to walk, both of us looking at the pictures on the wall.

'No, Tilly. I'm not. I live in an old wrecked building, I wash in the leisure centre and use public toilets, and I live for annoying the shite out of bigots, playing music and meeting interesting people.' He took my hand again and we both stopped walking. 'I don't want to be normal. I want to be here, like this. With you.'

He leant in and I did too and as our mouths touched he put his hand on my waist and I moved closer so that it went around my back, and I embraced him too, and we were like that for ages until it was time to breathe.

'Well, I suppose I'm happy not to be normal too,' I said.

He smiled and turned back to the painting.

'Halfway through,' he said. He continued the story, telling me about the first time they got involved in a 'mission' to help someone. 'It was an accident really,' he said. 'We just wanted to have fun. To party any time there was a riot – to take full advantage of the situation out there. Someone should be having fun while the city's burning outside, right? Well, then there was this one night. Seany was late, and when he showed up he was bleeding . . . '

'Wait – he's not here tonight, is he?'

Brew sighed. 'Naw. He's probably in the middle of the riot.'

'Seriously?'

'Yeah. It's what I was saying. That night he was late and bleeding – someone had chucked a brick at his sister, so he chucked one back and so on, and eventually one hit him.'

'His sister? Why?'

'Wrong place, wrong time? They live right on the corner where it all kicks off. Hard to avoid when it's literally on your doorstep. Anyway, he shows up, raging, says that he's gonna go out and kill the guy that did it, like, literally kill him.'

'Did you believe him?'

'Yeah. That's how it happens. Someone hits you, you hit back, and eventually you can't hit any harder.'

There was a pause. Brew looked serious, staring at the picture of Seany, bleeding, like he was looking through him to see something else.

'So, what did you do?' I asked, breaking his thought.

'Oh. We fed him a load of drink, kept him here until he fell asleep. And then we slashed his tyres.'

His face brightened, clearly pleased with the memory. He went on, 'Poor Seany. Woke up here the next afternoon, nursing the mother of all hangovers, got outside to jump on his auld bike and the thing was wrecked. He took one look at it, did a quick calculation about how long it'd take to go over and beat this guy's brains in and how possible it would be to get back out of the area alive afterwards, and thought better of it. He went back home to bed and came round here that evening ready to kill all of *us!*'

'Were you not a bit scared?'

'Of Seany?' He laughed hard. 'Naw. He's not a psycho, like. Few beers and he forgave us. He knew we'd saved his skin really.'

We were halfway down the line of pictures. In the next one Brew was kissing someone. I hoped he couldn't see my face getting hotter as we looked at it.

'A girlfriend?' I asked.

'Nope,' he said. 'First boyfriend.'

'Oh!' I hadn't expected it. 'Are you . . . ?'

'Bi,' he said. He turned to me. 'Does it bother you?'

I thought about it.

'No. And actually, I think that maybe I'm . . . bisexual too.'

He smiled.

'Cool.'

'Is it?'

He shrugged.

'Why not?'

'I dunno. I've never said that out loud before. I've actually never really thought about it before.'

'Well, there are no rules. You don't have think about it. You just like who you like, don't you?'

He definitely did see me going red then because he put his hand to my face and mimed getting burned. He was loving it.

'Do you like me, Tilly?'

'Isn't it obvious?'

'No, not really. I mean, I told you I liked you right from the start. But you've never said it to me. And in fact, I don't know anything about you, and now you know loads about me.'

God. What was I going to tell him? That I lived with a journalist who was gunning for him and his mates and would do everything he could to expose them if he knew that I'd been here for a couple of seconds, let alone hanging out with them all evening and kissing a guy wearing make-up in a dark tunnel? I checked my phone. We really needed to be getting back soon.

'Somewhere else to be?' Brew teased.

'Look, I'm really sorry, Brew, but Beth and I will have

to leave soon. I'm kind of responsible for bringing her here tonight and if I get into trouble she will too.'

'That's cool. She your best friend, then?'

'Yeah. She's been really good to me. Do you think the riot will have died down now?'

'If it has then you'll know because Seany will be here just as everyone's packing up. We'll go and check it out. You OK?'

'Yes, but I can't be late back.'

'You gonna turn into a pumpkin or something?'

I thought of Dad, who knew nothing about any of this. I thought of the stories in his paper and Brew's story on the wall and how they could never, ever touch something as real and true as what he'd done.

'Something like that, yeah.'

# Chapter 22

There were still plenty of people in the big courtroom. I looked around for Seany but I couldn't see him.

'Hey.' Brew nudged me. 'There he is.'

Seany was talking to the biker gang, who were laughing at whatever he was saying. He was buzzing, bouncing on his toes, drinking something from one of the mugs. He had a dark wound on the side of his head which he kept touching every so often.

'He's bleeding,' I said.

'He'll be grand. Lived to fight another day,' said Brew. 'And it means the riot's nearly over so we'll be finishing up here in a bit.'

'Doesn't rioting go against all that stuff youse do, though? I mean, he actually is doing wrong stuff, isn't he?'

'As opposed to living in a building that isn't yours and writing on other people's walls?'

I shrugged. I knew what he meant. But it was different – hurting people. It seemed like the opposite of the other stuff.

'Look,' said Brew. 'We're outsiders. We don't ask your religion or your politics or how much money you have in the bank. Sean has his own shit to deal with and, yes, he's living dangerously, but he's better with us than on his own. He knows that too.'

'But if people knew – about him – they might think that all of you . . . '

'You can't live by what other people might think. You just have to do what's right and live your life.'

*That's easy for him to say*, I thought. He doesn't have a dad who could extend their control of your life to the biggest national newspaper. He was free. I wasn't. But then again, I didn't have to think about riots or how to stop my friends from killing people.

'Aren't you frightened by the stuff you do sometimes? Like, when the cops are chasing you and stuff,' I said.

'Not when the cops are chasing us, no,' he said. 'That's sort of fun if I'm honest.'

'But the stuff you do – like at the rally with those blokes. It's dangerous, isn't it? If they'd caught you . . . '

He smiled. 'C'mere, I forgot something.' He led me back towards the tunnel.

'I really have to start getting home.'

'This'll only take a second. It's important,' he said.

He wanted me to understand, and so I followed him to a section of the mural near the beginning.

'Look at this.'

It was a picture of a rabbit, bum in the air, diving into a hedge.

'So I was walking home one night . . . '

'Home? You mean, here?'

'Yeah, that's what I said. I was walking home, and there was this car on the road. A small one. Ford Fiesta or something like that. It was driving along and there was this big lorry.' He spread out his hands. 'A huge big juggernaut, totally up its ass, right?'

'I hate that.'

'Yeah, what a twat! Anyway, I watched it. It tailgated this tiny little car the whole way up the street. And then' – he pointed to the rabbit – 'this fella here just casually hops out, right in front of the wee car.'

'Oh!'

'Yeah. So the small car stops to let it past and it took for ever. Hop. Stop. Hop. Stop. And all the time the guy in the small car is just waiting for it to cross. And of course the guy in the lorry was going totally nuts. Honking the horn, flashing his lights, being a real dick.'

'Scary.'

'I know! But still, whoever was driving the car in front just sat there. The bunny crossed the road, hopped into the hedge of someone's garden, the driver started up and continued on his way.'

'Wow. Good on them!'

'Right? The lorry guy flashed his lights on and off until I couldn't see them any more.'

'What a complete tool.'

'I know.' He shrugged his shoulder. 'Thing is, nobody would have given a shit if that bunny lived or died. Nobody, except that driver.'

'And the bunny.'

'Exactly.'

We stood there for a moment longer. I thought I understood him. Maybe. Was he the bunny, or the driver? Maybe both. I knew he wasn't the lorry guy.

'Anyway,' he said. 'Isn't scaling massive cranes a bit dangerous too?'

He had a point.

'And I'm not even doing that to help anyone,' I said, suddenly feeling completely self-centred.

'Yeah you are. You're doing it to help you.'

'Heh, that's true, I am.'

'That's a good thing, you know. Most people don't know how to help themselves. Most people just go to pieces.'

I looked at him as he stared at his rabbit, ducking into the hedge. I wondered what a person had to go through to know that most people just go to pieces. I felt very young beside him.

I looked at my phone again. We had fifteen minutes, tops. I'd better find Beth.

As I looked around for her, the crowd began to whistle and cheer. Someone was standing behind the judge's podium with one arm outstretched, holding the little hammer that a judge uses to declare the verdict. The other hand was holding a mask to their face. It was the beautiful floral skeleton face of Santa Muerte. I knew that it must have been Meg. She was wearing a long-sleeved red silk gown covered with sequins. There were peacock feathers in her hair and as she lowered the mask to applause, her mouth smiled widely through bright ruby lipstick.

I caught Beth's eye and beckoned her over. She hugged the girl she was with and came to stand beside me.

'Have you enjoyed it?' I whispered.

'Oh my God, so much!' said Beth, grinning widely. 'I can't wait to tell you about everyone I met.'

'Welcome! You are welcome!' Meg shouted through the increasing cheers. She waved her hands to cut through the noise, and the room was quickly calm. As she spoke, Brew left my side to walk to the front of the room and pick up a guitar. Scar did the same and I could see Sara picking up a bass guitar. As they arranged themselves, Meg was talking and throwing out her arms as if she had flowers to throw to the crowd, who were mesmerised and clapping on every pause.

'People of Belfast! Beautiful, human people! Thanks for joining us this evening! I want to invite some of my friends to join me in a song to mark the end of our evening, as the ministers of peace outside will soon return to the work of spoiling our fun. Please go home knowing that this too is your home, and knowing that they can never kill that which unites us. Love! And peace! And more love! And more love!'

As she repeated the words, the bass guitar began to pulse. Sara nodded her head to Scar and Brew, who began to add to the rhythm. A couple of people began to hit guitar cases and tables with the heels of their hands, a slow reggae rhythm, and then Meg began to sing.

It was a song about unity; I knew it from the radio. She was repeating the chorus over and over – telling us there was only one love, one song, one heart. Telling us we should give thanks.

Before long I knew the words, and everyone else knew them,

and we sang it together, and we clapped in time with the bass guitar, and sang it over and over and soon the musicians had stopped and wandered off, and Meg had stopped and was standing just smiling at everyone and we were all still singing and I felt a hand in mine and it was Beth. Her eyes were wet and I felt another hand in my other, and it was Brew, and then I felt like crying too because it felt like I'd been here for years, not hours, and everyone in the room was holding hands and singing then, and I knew, I knew that I was included in the 'us', that I was one of us.

# Chapter 23

It should have been a good day. A day where we floated along on the high of the previous evening, gossiping and going over everything, dissecting who said what and how they looked when they said it and how we felt about it all. But that's not how it turned out. I didn't even get to say good morning to Beth before my phone woke us both up. It was 9 a.m. We had planned to sleep until 10, shower quickly and run into school in time for second class.

'No idea,' I said, looking at the unknown number. I almost switched it off. Every part of my body wanted to melt back into the duvet. But I did answer it.

'Tilly? Is that you?'

'Yeah. Who's this?' I sat up and rubbed my eyes. I knew the voice but it wasn't anyone I'd spoken to on the phone before.

'It's Scar. Have you seen Brew? He's missing.'

'What? What do you mean?'

Beth sat up too.

'Who is it?' she hissed.

I ignored her. How could Brew be missing? We'd just seen him a few hours ago. He walked us home and I assumed he was going straight back.

'He's gone, Tilly. I was hoping he might've gone off with you?' Scar's voice was gentle but his words were coming out in a rush. 'We haven't seen him since youse left. It's not like him . . .'

'Maybe he just continued walking after he dropped us off? To walk off the beer?'

'Who went out for a walk?' Beth whispered. 'Is everything OK?'

I waved at her to shut up.

'No,' said Scar, 'he's always back by morning. Always. It's like a rule we have. Meg's frantic. She called me at work.'

'You have a job?'

'What? Yes, I have a job. And a flat. And a hamster, for God's sake, but look, if you see him will you let me know?'

'OK, don't panic. I'm sure he'll be OK.'

This was Brew, right? Brew, who could outrun the cops. Brew, who clowned about in front of bigots. Brew, who wasn't afraid to stand in front of juggernauts.

'I'm worried about him, Tilly,' said Scar.

I didn't get it. What was there to be afraid of? He was the most confident and capable person I'd ever met. And surely Scar knew him better than I did? Maybe that was it, though. Maybe there were things I didn't know.

Beth had stopped pestering me for information but she was boring a hole into my brain with her eyes. And I had to get off the phone or we'd be late. And now Scar was making me worried. What did he know that I didn't?

'Can I meet you after school? I could come over to where you work.'

'OK. It's Skull Happy.'

'The tattoo place?'

'Yeah.'

'Look, don't worry about him. I bet by the time I see you he'll be back again.' But I could hear how my voice had changed. I wasn't convincing myself, never mind Scar.

'I hope so. Look, thanks. I know we don't know each other all that well, and I don't mean to involve you in ... stuff ... but ... '

I waited. But what?

'Well,' he continued, 'I know Brew likes you. And he doesn't just trust anyone. I think he might contact you. Maybe. I mean, I hope so.'

'I hope so too.'

Beth pointed to her wrist, indicating that we needed to move it.

'I'll see you later, Scar.'

Beth's jaw dropped 'Scar?' she mouthed.

'OK. Thanks, Tilly. I really appreciate it.'

He hung up and I looked at the phone. Time for a lightning-fast shower.

'I'll explain on the way to school,' I told Beth.

'OK,' she said. Neither of us said a word more. We both knew something was up but neither of us knew what, and it was going to be a very long day waiting to find out.

# Chapter 24

I had never been to a tattoo place before. Beth came with me. I could see that she was a bit scared by the place. She drew her cardigan around her as if it would shield her from whatever germs she imagined were lurking in the dark corners of the polaroid-lined corridors. It was hard not to stare like a little kid. Hundreds, maybe thousands of photographs were stuck all over the walls. An angel. A panther. Darth Vader. A naked woman. Each one of them an image freshly torn into varying shades of white skin, each black outline bearing a red raw halo.

'How long do you think this will take?' whispered Beth.

'You don't have to stay with me, Beth. It's really fine.' I tried not to sound annoyed but she knew I was worried about Brew. I could really do without her adding to the stress. She didn't reply so I assumed she'd got the message.

'Can I help you?' A tall girl with sullen black lips, the bottom one pierced with a ring, was looking at us like we'd been aiming for Toys R Us and gotten horribly lost. I tried being brave. Sometimes lipstick's the only thing that disguises the fact that

111

we're all pretty boring really. Right? And piercings ... several piercings. Including one right through her cheek. And a tattoo of some kind of horrific demon on her forearm. She rolled her eyes and I realised that I hadn't answered her.

'Oh, uh, sorry. I'm here, we're here, to see Scar. He's expecting us.'

She pointed behind her with her thumb without looking round or saying a word and Beth and I moved towards the curtain at the back of the shop. There was no door so I couldn't knock but I could hear the whizz and squeal of the tattoo machinery.

'Go on, then!' whispered Beth as we stood outside the room.

'There might be someone, you know, getting a tat done.'

'Well du-uh, it's a tattoo parlour, isn't it?'

'I know, but what if they're not getting it done on their arm!'

'Eh?'

'What if they're having it done ... you know, in a private place?'

Beth burst out laughing and that was it – our cover was blown. The curtain flew back and there was Scar, who smiled widely to see us, transforming the dark room into a much warmer place.

'I'm so glad to see you! Hang on a bit.'

The man sitting opposite Scar said an awkward 'Hello' and winced as Scar finished off the tattoo on his hand; a soft, white flower.

'It's a lily,' he said. 'For my daughter.'

'Is she called Lily?' said Beth.

'No.' He looked confused. 'She's called Caitlin.'

'Oh. Right,' said Beth. 'Well, that's lovely.'

I could see Scar smirking, which made me want to laugh too. But I knew that in a minute the man would leave and I wanted it to be sooner because I needed to know what was going on. Was Brew back? Was there any news? I guessed that Scar felt the same because when he finished the tattoo he politely-but-swiftly ushered Caitlin's da out of the shop and changed the sign on the door to *Closed: Open again tomorrow for your pleasure, and pain.*

'OK, Caz. You can knock off early if you like – I need to talk to these two.'

Caz smiled through her deathly lipstick. Her eyes sparkled. It was like someone coming back to life. When she had gone, Scar flicked the switch on the kettle on the counter and indicated a couple of sofas where we could sit.

'I take it you haven't heard from him?' he said as we sat down.

'No. I take it you haven't either?'

'Nope. Not a word.' He sighed deeply. 'Tea OK?'

We both nodded. I could sense that this wasn't going to be the easy-going kind of conversation we'd had before in the courthouse. But I was determined that I wasn't going to leave without knowing what was going on. Scar handed us the mugs and sat down.

'Again, I'm sorry about this morning. I didn't mean to worry you ...'

To see someone like Scar looking like that – his big dark eyes heavy with tiredness or sadness, someone normally so joyful and animated now calmed and sitting, his big bear shoulders hunched over his cup of tea – I had to stop myself from giving him a hug.

'It's OK,' I said softly. 'Scar, what's going on? Do you know something? Do you know where he might be?'

He set down his cup and looked away from us, focusing on the portrait behind us of the naked back of a woman decorated with snakes and stars.

'OK,' he said at last. 'This is not an easy thing to say, because it might not be what has happened and I really hope it isn't what has happened, and I don't want to worry you any more, but it's a real possibility, and I suppose that if you're getting involved with Brew then . . .'

'Just tell us!' Beth spat out.

I would've given her a glare but I was glad she said it because it was what I had wanted to say too.

The UV light flickered slightly. I sipped my tea, holding the cup with both hands to stop it from shaking.

And so, he told us. He told us how Brew's family had been involved with paramilitaries since he could remember, how his mum was an alcoholic and her only way to survive was by doing favours for 'the boys', how it was manageable when Brew was little but when he got older there was a problem. The 'boys' wanted him to join their gang – to get involved in their 'activities'. First it was just hiding stuff or taking a package from here to there – no questions asked. But then they started asking him to join them on their outings. He didn't want to go but his mum made him because she needed everything to stay stable, so he went this one time and he saw a guy getting beaten up with wooden bats, and after that he didn't want to do it any more but his mum was pressuring him, and the lads were pressuring him; they were his friends, they said, but he knew that if he kept refusing they wouldn't always be his friends. And he'd seen what happens when friends turn into enemies. So he ran away and he met Meg and he'd started this whole other life away from them. But it wasn't enough. He couldn't cope with thinking about his mum and how she hadn't protected him and how she thought she didn't have a choice. So he decided he would have choices and he would choose differently.

'The missions?' I asked.

'Yes,' said Scar. 'But the lads back home weren't pleased about it.'

'How did they know?'

'Because a lot of the time the missions were against them.'

I couldn't believe it. He'd gone back to them. Right back to the same place to do crazy stunts. 'Why? To make a point? But why would he . . . ?'

'No. Not to make a point. To help people like him. There was always another person involved. Like Seany. They were neighbours before. Good mates.'

It made sense. But what was Scar saying? Where was Brew now? Beth had been thinking the same thing.

'Have these guys got him now, Scar? Have they kidnapped him?' she asked.

Scar shrugged.

'I don't know,' he said. 'But we had always worried about it happening. They really hate him. He fucks up loads of their plans. Makes them look like idiots, you know?'

The wrinkles on his brow made him look like an old man.

'One time there was this family who some of the boys wanted put out of the estate because they were Polish ... '

'That's so racist!' said Beth, open-mouthed.

'Yeah,' said Scar, amused by her shock, 'Brew thought so too. He organised us a huge gang to take it in turns sitting outside the family's house. Every night until the threat had died down and they moved on to annoy some other poor bastard.'

'So the family got to stay?'

'Yeah. They stayed until they could move somewhere else. They got a few threat-free months at least.'

The tea was freezing now and none of us had drunk it. Scar got up and flicked the kettle on again, as if tea was going to be the magic potion that made us all feel better.

'They never forgot that Brew had done it, though,' he carried on. 'Every so often they'll let him know that they're biding their time. Waiting for the right moment to get him.'

'That's so awful!' said Beth. 'He must be terrified all the time!'

Scar sighed, dipping fresh tea bags into cups of boiling water.

'I wish he was a bit more terrified, to be honest.' He handed up fresh mugs of boiling tea. 'But that's Brew. He doesn't worry about himself much.'

The tea burned my hands through the Sex Pistols mug.

'Who are they?'

He shook his head. 'I can't tell you that, Tilly. These aren't just kids – they're men. It's a serious organisation.'

'Why can't you tell me? You know. And I bet Meg knows, right?'

'Sorry. It's best you don't know who they are.'

*So I'm in but I'm not 'in',* I thought. It stung a little. But I pushed it out of my thoughts.

'What can we do?' I asked Scar.

'All we can do is wait,' he said. 'And hope that we're wrong.'

'What might they do to him?' said Beth.

I wished she hadn't asked because I was trying not to imagine it.

'Anyone's guess,' said Scar. 'But they really don't like him . . . '

He was trying not to imagine it too.

'If it hadn't been for me,' I began.

'Shush,' said Scar. 'Don't be thick.'

'No, I mean, if he hadn't been walking me home . . . then he'd be OK, wouldn't he?'

Scar shook his head. 'Don't do that, Tilly. Brew's his own person – he goes out at night all the time – this isn't your fault.'

Beth put her arm around me.

'Look,' she said, 'we shouldn't jump to conclusions. It's only been a day – not even a whole day – he might've just, I dunno, gone off for a bit. The party was intense. Maybe he needed his head showered.'

Who was she kidding? My mind was racing. I was picturing him lying at the side of the road, bleeding, run over by the juggernaut, and who was there to stand in its way for Brew?

# Chapter 25

It was the following evening before I heard the news. I had been trying not to obsess about him, and failing. Beth had tried to cheer me up in the canteen. We were talking about our media homework – a study of sexism in some film or other – and she could tell I wasn't listening.

'Your life would fail the Bechdel test, you know,' she said, stirring her tea.

'Huh?'

'Huh?' she said, mocking me.

'Sorry,' I said. 'I can't concentrate on anything . . . '

'I know. That's what I mean.'

'What?'

'Ever since you met Brew, that's all you think about.' She smiled but she was serious. Maybe she was just worried that I was getting so involved with this missing person who was always in danger, but it felt like she was having a go at me.

'That's not true.'

It was true. It bothered me that it was true. I wished that

I didn't care so much. I wished that I wasn't so worried. But it was rude of her to point it out. 'And anyway,' I continued, 'what about when you and Mr Tennis Club were a thing? I had to endure endless blahing on about that didn't I?'

'I suppose so.' She stopped smiling and I felt a bit crap about it. She had broken up with Daniel a few days after the party and I wasn't missing hearing about her boring problems with him, but maybe I didn't have to be so blunt.

'Sorry.'

'It's OK,' she said. 'You're right. We're both rubbish feminists.'

It made me laugh but maybe there was a hint of truth in it. I hadn't done my media homework. I didn't even know what the Bechdel test was. Something about films and women obsessing over men all the time? I had worried my way through the last couple of days, letting everything that every teacher said float over my head to the person behind me. All I could think about was Brew, and where he was, and if he was OK. It was making me crazy. But I couldn't help it. Could I? The bell went and we stood up.

'I haven't done the media, Beth.'

'At all?'

'None of it. And I haven't done the history assignment either.'

'Oh God, he's gonna kill you. He'll phone your dad.'

'I know. I'm going to try and get it done tonight.'

'All of it? That's mad. It's three thousand words for the history alone.'

'I know.' We crossed the corridor towards history. 'But I'll pull an all-nighter and get it done. It'll be shit, but I'll get it done.'

Beth rolled her eyes.

'You should've said you were behind. I could have helped you.'

She would have too. We had always helped each other out like that. One time I spent the whole weekend at her house, nights too, helping her with a music exam piece. But the truth was that this time I hadn't even been thinking about the assignment. I had let Brew and Scar and the gang dominate my every thought and I filed everything else away in a part of my brain marked 'later'. And now it was later, and I was behind, and Dad might find out and want to know why.

Beth and her sarcastic comment had snapped me out of it, maybe just in time. I'd get the work done. I'd make an excuse for why it was crap and I'd make sure it never happened again. I'd put Brew in the 'later' file and I'd force myself to think of him only after I had done the other stuff. I knew if I didn't then Dad would find out. As I walked home that afternoon I told myself over and over that Brew wouldn't have been this worried about me. Would he? Think about it. He was happy enough to let me go when I said I didn't want to see him. He wouldn't tell me about his past life – Scar had to do that. He kept things for himself so why couldn't I? And he'd been living on his own in a squat for ages – surely he could look after himself. He didn't need me.

I repeated it to myself as I crossed the road: *he doesn't need me.* As I passed a crowd of kids piling on to a bus: *he doesn't need me.* As I rounded the corner into our development: *he doesn't need me.*

And as I drew nearer to our house I tried a new mantra: *and I don't need him. I don't need him. I don't need him.*

It was fifteen minutes later, as I was carrying a mug of tea up to my room, with every intention of focusing on the French Revolution, when my phone rang. I looked at the number. Scar. I set down the tea and sat on my bed. *Please let it be good news. Please.*

'Hi. Did you find him? Is he OK?'

'Yes.' His voice was quiet. 'Yes, we found him.'

There was a pause and in that silence my resolve vanished. I couldn't ask. I wanted to, but I couldn't. Scar eventually spoke again.

'He's alive. But they beat the shit out of him.'

'Oh. Oh God.'

'I hate being the one to tell you, Tilly. You know, you don't have to be part of this – he knew it was on the cards and he didn't tell you – so it's OK if you walk away. He . . . he told me to tell you that.'

'You've seen him? Where?'

'He's in the Royal. He doesn't want any visitors – he's pretty messed up . . . '

'What do you mean?'

'Mashed-up face. Few broken teeth. Think his legs are just bruised, not broken. But they tried. Broken rib. Stitches in his head . . . '

'Shit.'

'Yeah.'

'But he's alive, though,' I said, trying to sound hopeful. 'Thank goodness.'

'Yeah.' Scar's voice was flat. 'They said they'd kill him next time.'

'Next time?'

'If he didn't stop it. If he didn't stop bothering them, in their area.'

'But he will, right?'

There was silence again. I couldn't believe what I wasn't hearing. Surely he wasn't going to continue to piss them off? I mean, it wasn't worth his life. And it was selfish of me, I know it was selfish, but I thought, what about me? Didn't he care – that I cared? What about his friends? Maybe he didn't deserve good friends if that's how he treated them. Us. I could hear Scar's breath. I wondered if he knew what I was thinking. I wondered if he had thought it himself.

'That's just how Brew is, Tilly,' he said. 'But he really won't hold it against you if you walk away. None of us will.'

'What ward's he in?'

'He doesn't want . . .'

'He doesn't get a choice. I'll decide if I want to stick around after I've spoken to him. What ward?'

'Eight.'

'Thanks. And thanks for calling.'

'No worries.'

I honestly don't know if it was sympathy or anger that made me cycle over to the hospital. Maybe both. Maybe they're part of the same thing. I knew I had to see him and I wanted to be raging. I wanted to shout and have nurses tell me off for disturbing the patients. I wanted to swear at him and tell him what a shitty time I'd had worrying about him, about how angry I was that I had to think about him all the time and not Napoleon or the bloody Bechdel test and how ironic it was that

I couldn't write an essay about women's oppression because I was too busy thinking about him even though he clearly couldn't give a tiny rat's ass about me.

By the time I got to the hospital doors I was buzzing with the energy of my anger. I wasn't going to get that school work done – I'd have to make up a lie about why, and I had to lie to Dad about going to the library. More lies, and all because of him, all because I couldn't stop myself from feeling connected to him. I punched the floor number on the lift. It wasn't fair and I wanted to tell him but more than anything I wanted not to feel like this – I wanted to let him go.

And then I saw him.

He was in a ward with five other beds in it. There was a curtain dividing him and the person next to him. He was lying very still and there were bandages and his face was not like his face. It was a dark rainbow of colour with Brew's eyes just about looking out through stitches and bruises and swelling. And all the feelings I had been having melted into tears and I could feel them falling from my cheeks.

'Hi,' he whispered.

I couldn't reply for a minute. He'd been flattened. Nobody but himself to help him. Confident, cocky, brave Brew. Where was he? Somewhere under those bandages. Somewhere that you couldn't recognise.

I sat on the chair beside his bed.

'They said I could only stay a minute.'

His face moved slightly into what might have been a smile. 'Thanks for coming.'

'Don't try to speak.' I could tell it was painful. 'You don't have to. I just came to ... Well, to be honest I came to yell at you.' It was meant to be a joke but it made me want to cry again. I swallowed the urge to let go. 'Anyway. We'll be able to talk properly soon.'

A nurse appeared at the side of the curtain.

'Sorry. Visiting hours are up now,' she said.

'OK.'

I got up. I didn't know what to do. I couldn't kiss his face. Every part of it looked like it might scream if I touched it. I couldn't take his hands as they were both in bandages. I put a hand lightly on his shoulder, as light as I could.

'I'll come back again. Get better soon.'

I hoped that he could sense everything through that touch. Whatever 'everything' was. The nurse smiled sympathetically and I left the room. Nobody else spoke to me as I left. They were all busy doing other things, like everyone in a hospital always is. Everyone except the patients. I thought that was it – I'd be alone with my confusing, crazy thoughts the whole way home. But as I got closer to the exit the door swung open and a woman in a leopard-print fake fur coat and black patent heels ran in.

'Tilly!'

Meg grabbed both my arms.

'I'm too late, aren't I? Are visiting hours over? Oh shit.'

Her face crumpled and I could see tears on her face behind her huge sunglasses.

'Oh, for God's sake. Look at the state of me!' She searched in her bag and found a crumpled silk hanky. Removing her shades and dabbing her eyes, she took a couple of deep breaths before gathering herself and forcing a smile.

'How are you, Tilly? Are you OK, love?'

'Yes. Are you?'

'Not really, love!' Her voice cracked a bit as she dabbed her eyes. 'Have you got time for a coffee?'

# Chapter 26

They could have made an effort to make the hospital canteen seem less like an actual hospital. White walls, stainless steel, hospital staff in various shades of hospital uniform. There wasn't even any art on the walls. But I don't think Meg noticed. She stirred and stirred her tea, her great fake fur coat hunched about her shoulders. I wondered what she'd look like in a tracksuit, like me. Or a T-shirt and jeans. Did she even own a pair of jeans? Would anyone who knew her recognise her without those rouged cheeks?

'I'm devastated, darling,' she said, finally. 'Poor Brew. He knew this might happen but he simply throws caution to the wind.'

'Yes,' I said, sipping my coffee. 'Maybe this will be a wake-up call though, eh?'

I was trying to offer her something: a way to feel relieved that Brew was at least still alive. But she looked confused.

'What do you mean?'

'Well, maybe he'll be more careful now. About where he does his missions, or whatever.'

Meg looked surprised. She rubbed her eyes.

'Oh, dear,' she said, softly. 'No, I don't think so.' She took my hand, the way a mother might if she was breaking bad news to her little girl. 'This isn't going to end up the way you hope.'

Now it was my turn to be confused. Didn't Meg want Brew to be safe? Surely that's why she took him in – helped him out with the squat? Isn't that what she was doing, with all of them? She saw my face and I knew she understood. She gave my hand a squeeze before letting it go and lifting her tea to her mouth.

'Yes. We look after one another,' she said. 'But what we have ... our group ... it's bigger than us. I know that you love him ...'

I almost dropped my coffee. 'Who said anything about ... ?'

'I can see that you do.' She smiled. 'And I think he loves you too, Tilly.'

No, I didn't. *He* didn't. This ... whatever it was ... this thing with him ... it wasn't even an official thing, was it? And we'd kissed, like, twice. And I still felt removed from him in a way that told me we weren't really 'together', not like couples that are together properly.

But I couldn't deny that I was sitting here in a hospital canteen instead of sorting out my studies. Or that I'd done more things in the last few weeks that would piss Dad off than in my whole life up to now. And I didn't have anything to compare it to. Is this what it's like – being in love? Just being stressed all the time? Thinking about the other one all the time to the point where I was morphing into the kind of girl I really didn't like in films or books? No, no. I didn't want to be that. And if he loved me, then ...

Meg broke my thoughts.

'I'm sorry, Tilly. Brew won't stop the missions. It would be like asking him not to be Brew. It's what he lives for – to reverse the actions of those people who tried to break him.'

'But, he's going to get . . . '

'It could happen.' There were tears in her eyes again. 'It could happen to any of us. But this thing – it's bigger than us.'

'What thing? What are you talking about? So what if you have a gang? Just do something else. Help people in another way! Who are these people anyway?'

Meg glanced around the room and although it was mostly empty I lowered my voice again.

'Who are they? You should tell someone!'

Meg shook her head. She was smiling but she seemed so sad.

'If he wanted out, I'd support him, in whatever way I could. And I could, Tilly. I've offered before. He could have the life that you'd like him to have. He could have a house, a job, two kids and a pet dog.'

'I don't want him to have . . . '

'I'd get him a proper place to live tomorrow,' she went on. 'But it's not his way. I can't go behind his back to the police. I don't have any evidence it was them, and you try asking Brew who did it. He won't tell you.'

What did she mean, she'd get him a proper place to live? Would she buy him a flat? And maybe I did want him to have a normal life. What was wrong with that anyway? He wouldn't have been beaten so badly that he couldn't speak now if he had a house and job and all that other stuff. I suddenly realised that maybe Dad had been right about the gang. But now I was in, wasn't I? Could I leave? It would mean leaving him. And lovely Scar. And Meg, Meg who seemed to care, but wasn't stopping it. And that's what parents were meant to do, wasn't it? They don't just let kids wreck their lives, do they? They try.

'You could try, Meg. You could try to stop him.'

She laughed gently.

'How would I do that? Lock him in the courthouse?'

'No ... but you could put pressure on him ... get everyone else to do it too.'

'Stage an intervention, love?' She sighed, clasping her cup. 'Brew's been on his own for a while. At first I wanted to save them all. I wanted to bring them all home. Give them a cosy room and a warm drink. Tuck them up, safe and warm, at night, like Heidi, or little orphan Annie.' She took my hand again. 'But in real life we can't control people, Tilly. We can only love them. It's the best we can do.'

A buzzer sounded and the people in uniforms got up sharply.

'I think that's our cue to leave,' said Meg. I looked at my phone. Shit. I'd think of something to say to Dad on the way home. And maybe I'd think about everything else too. About what to do. And how to love a person who wants to stand in front of juggernauts. Maybe Meg was right – maybe this thing, whatever it was, was bigger than me. The only things I knew for sure were that I was glad Brew was alive, and I was confused about everything else, and that my essay wasn't going to get done in time for class tomorrow.

# Chapter 27

Text message from Beth. 11.15 a.m.:

> **Thought maybe you were going be late to class ... but it's break time and you're not here? Take it you didn't pull an all-nighter and do the history then??? Any news about Brew?**

I sat up in bed. It was time to get up. Dad had asked if I wanted him to stay at home after I told him I was sick. He seemed relieved when I croaked that I thought I would be fine, I just needed to rest and I was sure I'd be fine for the next day. Or maybe the day after that. He went off to work at the usual time saying that he'd phone later to check I was OK. He wasn't even suspicious. And that's what made me feel terrible. This wasn't me, really. Mitching off school because I hadn't done the work, my head full of boys and gangs. I knew that Beth would have me sussed but it was still annoying that she did. I was beginning to regret introducing her to everyone.

It wasn't my secret any more. I couldn't even lie about school without her knowing pretty much exactly what was going on. The only thing she didn't know about was the climbing and although I had totally planned to spend the whole day getting caught up with history and media, I had already spent the first three hours since Dad left drifting in and out of sleep and thinking about whether or not I should climb something today – try to collect my thoughts, make a plan. Beth's text woke me up properly.

> You got me, I typed. I'm staying in to do it today. I need to get caught up on loads of stuff. They found Brew. He got beat up but he'll be OK.

I sent the text, got up and got straight into the shower. When I had finished there was another text waiting for me from Beth,

> So ... what were you doing last night if you weren't working? Were you with him?

I decided not to answer that one. This was going to be a non-Brew day. I had decided in the shower. I'd make a pot of tea and sit down with Napoleon. I was going to switch off my phone too. Maybe tonight I'd go out and climb something, after dark, but today was about putting things right with school stuff. I could totally do it in one day, I wasn't that much behind, and I'd just have to make sure it didn't happen again.

And it was hard, but that's what I did. I wouldn't say

the essay was brilliant, but it was passable – something you wouldn't be too suspicious about. And I read up on all the media stuff and found out what the Bechdel test was. I was right, it was about films. Your film would pass the test if two female characters had a conversation about something other than a man. It made me smile. Beth was right. But I was going to change now.

By 5 p.m. I had all my work up to date, more or less, and I felt like myself again. I could handle this thing with Brew. I could see him and study. I could keep my distance, not get too involved, let him go his own way. After all, I wasn't really part of their gang – I didn't have to go on their missions. I could just be there for, like, moral support or something. My life was different to theirs. I had school to think about, and Dad. Beth was able to join in with them and not get too involved, so why couldn't I do that too?

I thought back to her text and decided to switch on my phone. There was about an hour before Dad got back. Time to kick back. Bit of telly, maybe. Cup of tea. I felt pretty pleased with myself, really.

Two messages. Beth and Brew. I took a deep breath.

Beth, 12.30 p.m.:

Hmmm. Not answering. Take it that means you were with Brew? Hope he's OK. Hope you know what you're doing . . . text me back or I'll think you've eloped with him and left me with the media assignment all on my own ☹

I decided to text her back before I read Brew's message:

> Sorry – not married – just switched phone off! Up to date
> with work. See you tomorrow. Everything's fine! ☹

And now for Brew's message. I fell backwards onto the bed and arranged the pillows under my head. I paused before tapping on his name.

Brew, 1 p.m.:

> Hey. Sorry I was so out of it last night. High as a kite on
> these painkillers. Thanks for coming to see me. Hope it
> didn't freak you out. I'm planning a thing for when I get out
> of here. It's gonna be brilliant. Speak to you soon Tilly? X

I read my own name, hearing it in Brew's voice, and felt the thing I had forgotten about all day. The off-beat thud in my chest. Not my heartbeat but something extra, like a second pulse. I rolled over onto my stomach and held the pillows over my head, scrunching my eyes shut so tightly that I could see tiny specks of lights and colours colliding like rainbow stars in the black sky. Shit. Shit. Shit. How can I not stop feeling like this? You have a plan, Brew? Good for you! I have a plan too. I plan to pass my exams and get out of this place – off somewhere to university, anywhere, but away. And that plan really never included getting my head beat in by a gang of idiot thugs, or my dad finding out in the daily police reports to his office that I'd been arrested.

Even so, as I tried to convince myself how mad it was, how childish it was, how stupid and reckless it was ... even so, the extra pulse was whispering something inside me and I couldn't shut it up. *What if? What if?* it said.

133

Dad's voice, Beth's voice, even my own rational voice ...
they were all on the outside. The voice inside me thrilled to
hear the sound of Brew saying my name, and I knew that I
would see him when he got out, and I knew his plan would be
something crazy and something great and that it would be a
plan about doing good, and I knew that I would want to be a
part of it because somehow Brew, and Meg, and Scar – somehow they were a part of me now, because I wanted them there.
That was the truth of it – I wanted to be with them, to be part
of them, I *felt* part of them. Suddenly I knew what Meg had
meant about it being bigger than them. Maybe this is what
having a religion is like – you're in it, even if you think it might
not be sensible. A religion. Or an addiction. Or a family.

I sat up. My head was banging. Love, Meg had said.

I really needed that cup of tea now.

# Chapter 28

At least school would be a Brew-free zone. The perfect excuse to keep my phone switched off and to think about other things. Important things, like study.

'So. Hands up. How many feminists do we have in the room?'

Paul Carr rolled his eyes and made a fake snoring noise.

'I take it we can discount you, Paul. Anyone else?'

Ms Thomson looked hopefully round the room. A few girls raised their hands. Beth put her hand up high. She nudged me.

'Come on!' she whispered.

I half raised mine. I wasn't really sure what it meant any more.

'Huh. Typical,' grunted Kyle McClelland. 'The fat lezzer and her best mate.'

There were a couple of giggles. Beth raised an eyebrow at me. I guess more people knew about me and Shauneen than I'd realised. The funny thing was that I really didn't care any more. I smiled at Shauneen to let her know that it didn't bother me if that's what people thought. The idea of being worried about getting caught doing something so innocent seemed childish now.

'You're such a 'phobe, Kyle,' said Jules Morgan. It got a bigger laugh than Kyle's comment. Shauneen smiled back at me.

'Yes,' said Ms Thomson. 'We can do without the casual homophobia, Kyle, thank you.'

'And misogyny, Miss,' said Jules.

'Yes. And thank you for leading us back to the subject, Jules. What *is* feminism in 2017?'

It was a pretty good discussion. I took some notes on the changes in twentieth-century feminism. Then Ms Thomson switched on the projector and asked someone to switch off the lights.

'In this short film you will hear a local woman talking about what feminism means to her today. Take notes – you might pick up something useful for your homework assignment.'

There was a collective groan as the film started. I was looking in my pencil case trying to decide whether to take the notes in black or green as the voice began to speak. I knew who it was before she had finished her introduction. Beth grabbed my arm.

'Hello. I am Elizabeth Mechtild Robinson-Fford and this is my home.'

The woman in front of the camera waved a braceleted arm behind her without looking. The house in the distance was huge and grey. Its windows glinted under a clear blue sky and the fountain at the end of the driveway gushed sparkling sunshine into a large pool of silver.

The woman smiled widely and went on.

'My friends just call me Meg, though.'

Neither Beth nor I could take our eyes off the screen.

'Some people think that if you're born into wealth you couldn't possibly be a feminist. After all, we have everything handed to us on a plate, don't we?'

She was loaded? And that house! My head was spinning. She had said something . . . about telling Brew she could sort him with a house and stuff . . . bloody hell. I thought that she'd meant helping him with rent somewhere, not buying him a mansion!

Meg went on to say how feminists could be from all walks of life. She moved through the grounds of her home as she spoke.

'When I was a young girl my mother used to tell me that women had the hardest lives in the world. Can you imagine sitting here, in this garden, listening to that?'

The garden Meg stood in was a carpet of colour. Long-stemmed purple flowers swayed beside red poppies, daisies, buttercups, exotic-looking green grass plants with pointy tips, tiny white flowers, huge black tulips . . .

'But she was right. What she was saying, really, was that I was not the only little girl in the world.'

Meg picked a daisy.

'She taught me to look at other women, and when I started doing that I began to see myself.'

She sat down on a low wall near a statue of a man carrying a jar on his shoulder.

'Nobody can be a feminist on their own. If you're a woman then you need other women. That's what it means to me, I suppose. We are important to one another, even if we don't realise it. And we don't need to be afraid of that. Feminism is bigger than us all.'

Meg smiled and looked off-screen as the picture faded out. Ms Thomson paused the film and the class sat in the dark in silence.

'Lights, please, someone?'

When the lights went on Beth turned to me, her face full of words. I wanted to talk about it too but we couldn't. Ms Thomson wanted us to write some notes in silence until the end of the lesson. I glanced at Beth's page after five minutes. She hadn't written a word and neither had I. What could I write? *I knew this woman who was a bit eccentric and she hung round with a gang who were also all a bit strange, and then it turned out she was way, way more different than I had thought ... and she's loaded ... and she lives in a house that looks like it fell out of a Jane Austen novel.*

Bloody hell. I thought of Meg in her colourful shawls and diamante heeled boots. Meg, addressing the outcasts of Belfast at an illegal party in a derelict building. Meg, handing round Brew's home-made lager. Meg, who seemed like a kind of mother to Brew, who spoke to you like you were an equal but who also made you feel like she was bigger than you, because of how she cared.

'Nothing to write, girls?'

Beth and I looked up at Ms Thomson. I was just about to mutter something about how I was still turning over the idea about feminism being women sticking together, when the bell went and chairs scraped and Ms Thomson started searching on her desk for our homework sheets. People were leaving as fast as they could before she found them and Beth and I grabbed our stuff and went for the door, packing our things away as we walked.

'I cannot believe it!' said Beth

'Me neither! I mean. I knew Meg was different, but . . . '

'But holy shit, Tills. She's rich! Like properly rich.'

'I know! I mean, it makes sense in a way. The other night she was saying how . . . '

'The other night? Were you with her?'

Crap. Now I was going to have to talk about Brew. Oh well, I suppose one more school corridor analysis of Me-and-Brew wasn't going to make much difference.

Beth and I walked to the lunch room as I began to fill her in on the hospital, Meg, Brew's text. As we sat down in our spot I noticed how little Beth was saying and how serious she looked. This was not going well.

'I know what you're going to say,' I said.

She didn't change her expression. She looked off to the side as if she was gathering her thoughts, preparing to say something full of wisdom. I waited. And then she spoke.

'You're acting like a real dick, Tilly.'

'What?' I was mid-slurp of my Fanta and I almost spat it out.

Beth shook her head.

'You are. Nobody else is going to tell you this so I have to.'

'What?' I said again. 'How am I a dick?'

'I didn't say you *were* a dick. I said you were *acting* like a dick.'

'What difference does that make?!'

She screwed the lid onto her drink and primly took a mouthful of tuna pasta.

'Actually,' she said, swallowing, 'it makes a big difference. It means you don't have to act that way. It means you can take responsibility. It means you have a choice.'

'A choice? I don't even know what you're talking about. I haven't done anything!'

Beth looked around and lowered her voice.

'A choice, to think about how Brew is negatively affecting your actual life. A choice to... woman-up.'

'To what?!'

'Stop saying "what". To woman up. It's like "man up" only not sexist, because obviously you're not a man, and anyway, being tough isn't ... '

'OK, spare me the feminism lecture. Could you just tell me what you're on about? How am I *acting like a dick*? And by the way, shouldn't it be *acting like a vagina*, if we're being so feminist about everything?'

A couple of Year Nines from the next table gawped at us. Beth smiled at me gently. I scowled back at her. My pasta was cold but I didn't feel like eating it anyway. Who did she think she was? Jeremy frickin' Kyle? I didn't need her life advice.

'Actually, no, it shouldn't be *acting like a vagina* because ... '

'I don't care!' I said, too loudly. The whole Year Nine table was looking at us now, waiting to see what was next. 'You're just pissed off because I didn't tell you about seeing Brew when you texted yesterday. I'm away,' I said, leaving my tray on the table and heading for the fire exit without looking back at Beth.

'Wait! Wait!'

She came after me but I didn't stop until I was outside and across the pitch and sitting on the wall at the far end of the school. We were alone now. The sky was grey and cold and the school bell was just minutes away. A handful of boys were milling around at the other end of the pitch, half-heartedly kicking a ball between them. Everything – all these kids in their uniforms, the blank-eyed walls of the school, the familiarity of bells ringing and locker doors slamming, and teachers squeaking their dried-out markers over the plastic of the whiteboards . . . and even Beth with her perfectly straight hair cut across the bottom in a perfectly straight line – all of it was moving further and further away in my mind from what seemed real.

Beth sat down beside me

'Are you OK?' she said.

I turned my face away from her.

'You're right,' she said. 'A bit. I did feel a bit shut out yesterday.'

I turned my face towards her again but I was still angry.

She tried a smile and slipped her arm through mine and I didn't pull away. 'I'm sorry for being so judgemental. I'm a bit worried about all this stuff with Brew. I thought it was over.'

'So did I.' My voice came out like a whisper.

Beth squeezed my arm.

'You're not really acting like a dick. Or a vagina.'

I laughed, despite myself, and Beth laughed too and she sounded like herself again. It was such a relief that it made me want to cry. And then I thought, what the hell? And so I did cry, and Beth didn't say anything else about feminism or dicks or vaginas, she just put her arm around me and we sat there and I had a quiet sob on her shoulder, and I don't even know why I was crying, I suppose it was just that everything was changing and it was good to know that some things are always the same.

# Chapter 29

On the top of Goliath, Samson's little brother, I sat, cross-legged and cold in the dark, remembering. It had been so long since my last climb that I had forgotten the thrill of hearing the blood in my ears as my breath became heavier the higher I got. About halfway up I would begin to climb in time with my pulse, everything moving together, towards the top. And the harder it became to keep going, the more I wanted to get there, because I knew I could, on my own. Just me, quietly beating in a dark corner of the city, in time with myself. And at the end – the top – stretching out, touching the sky a little closer, as close as possible. I wondered why so few people did it.

In an hour I would be meeting Brew at the Ark Cafe, just like our first meeting. I tried to remember not knowing him or Meg or the others. But I couldn't. And it was OK. I had told Beth about how I was feeling and she had promised to help me keep my grades from completely crashing as long as I kept myself safe. I wondered if she'd think I was safe now, so high above the concrete floor of Belfast. She'd probably worry less about me doing this than hanging around with the gang. Dad too. But I wasn't about to let them know. I was going to do this for ever. Perhaps until I fell off. Maybe everyone has something in them that they need to do until the very end.

The street lights began to pick out a pattern below me. I wondered who was down there. Were any of them wondering who was up here? *As long as I have this*, I thought, *it will be OK. Whoever gets into trouble, whatever my exams turn out like, there'll always be something to climb and a place to go where there's just me and the wind.*

A seagull squawked behind me. I turned around and it picked at the steel rivets of the crane for a minute before disappearing into the black. I lay down on my back. The lights of the town gave the edges of the night an orange glow, and a silver wisp of cloud was spun around the sky like candyfloss. Time to go.

Brew was already at the Ark. I could see him inside as I approached, sitting forward on his seat, stirring his coffee. He didn't look like he'd been beaten up or left for dead. A few bruises on his face, but nothing really looked any different to that first night when I'd met him here. But everything had changed. I wasn't going to meet a stranger now. And for the first time I wasn't nervous about seeing him.

His face broke into a grin as he noticed me at the window. He stood up and beckoned me in and I grinned back, and within seconds we were on the inside, together, hugging one another, a kiss on the cheek, and that was it. 'I missed you,' he said. And then we were chatting about everybody and about coffee and about the random exchange he'd witnessed in the town between a man and his dog earlier, and that girl who worked for Scar and ... everything. It was normal, and real, and warm. I found myself thinking that if Dad really knew Brew that he'd like him, and then I tried to unthink it because I could never imagine Brew coming round to ours for tea and making polite conversation with my dad. So nothing was perfect. So what? This moment was ours and it was good, and I was ready to hear about the new plan and I was sure I could handle it, whatever it was, I knew I was ready for it.

I thought I knew.

# Chapter 30

'So, that's it. Whadeya think?'

'I think you're nuts.'

Brew smiled like it was the greatest compliment. He looked at his phone.

'There's time for another coffee. What are you having?'

He was on his feet and heading to the counter.

'Cappuccino?' I said.

He had a slight limp.

I was unsure if he'd heard but it didn't matter. I sank back on my seat. The Maze prison? It was miles away. How were they expecting to get all the way out there? Maybe Meg was going to drive? She probably had a fleet of limos or something. Haha, imagine them all showing up at the derelict prison site in stretch limousines with their spray cans and paintbrushes. But even if they were able to get there, it was a mad idea. The Maze prison, or Long Kesh as it was known, hadn't been used since the Troubles ended and the prisoners were released. Parts of it had been pulled down. It would definitely be locked up. Parts of it might be dangerous, even. And even if they got in and started doing their graffiti or whatever, so what? There'd be nobody there to see it, would there? Seemed like an awful lot of trouble for no good reason, but Brew was really excited about it.

Brew returned with both coffees and a chocolate brownie which he cut in half, pushing one piece towards me.

'Cheers,' I said, breaking a bit off. He looked at his phone again.

'You expecting a call?' I said.

'What? Ah. No. Just watching the time.'

'Am I keeping you back? I can go home – I have homework anyway.'

'Oh. I was kind of hoping you'd come with me, actually. But if you're busy ... '

'Well ... I do have homework. But I have a study double tomorrow ... Why, where are you going? Is it about the Maze prison thing?'

'No, no. Although I hope you're going to come on that little adventure as well?'

I smiled without answering and swallowed the last bit of brownie. I wanted to go. Even if the idea seemed mad: to take over the prison, to decorate it all, to make something of it rather than letting it go to ruin.

'So what's tonight, then?'

Brew lifted his phone again and started tapping on it. Then he handed me the handset. It was a list of messages on a social media site. Hundreds of them. I scrolled down. They all had the same hashtag, #BELFIST2.

@weejonny735 See youse then. Better be ready. #BELFIST2

@janetison 8pm watch that wee doll get her head bate in yeoooo! #BELFIST2

@offmahead Nearly time melters! Don't forget the carryouts. #BELFIST2

'Oh my God, Brew, what is this?'

'Planned fight. Second of the year. East Park. Gonna be a belter by the sounds of it.'

He took his phone back and put it in his pocket.

'What? I mean – what are you going to do? Watch it? Or . . . or are you gonna fight? Are these the ones that beat you up? Are you fucking in*sane*?'

He was holding back laughter.

'Neither, you doofus. I'm a lover, not a fighter. You coming?'

And he stood up and put on his coat and I had to decide, right then. I was a lover not a fighter too, wasn't I? But if that was true then how come we were walking towards a fight and not running far away from it? But we left the Ark. Side by side and away from peaceful people having cosy chats over tea and cake, out into the breeze again, along the docks in the dark. He took my hand and for a minute I imagined that we were just lovers, on a romantic stroll watching the boat masts jab the black night. It was never going to be like that with Brew, though – we were never going to be 'just' anything. We'd always be walking towards a fight. A shiver thrilled the length of my spine. We left the docks and headed towards East Park.

At the gates to the park, Meg and Scar stood together facing

148

out into the street, chatting and laughing. When they saw us, Meg clapped her hands and held out her arms and Scar joined in the group hug. You'd've thought we were all going for a night out on the town rather than heading towards some mass punch-up.

'My *God*, you two look *great!*' said Meg, looking at Brew and me.

'Oh, cheers love!' said Scar, arms folded, faking a huff. Seeing them again made me wonder why I'd been so determined to give them a miss.

'Don't worry, Scar,' I said, taking his arm as we walked into the park. 'We all know you're the sexy one.'

'Watch it!' said Brew, laughing.

We carried on like that across the pitches, along the flowered border of the duck pond, and out onto the rough path that led to the kids' play park. Beth and I used to come here when we were little. Not much had changed. There were a few more notices up now about health and safety, and a bit more graffiti, but the old stinky toilet block was still there, and the dried-up fountain, and as we approached the floodlit play area I could see that all the old equipment was still there. But now the tube slide had four big kids sitting on top of it, and there were more teenagers, everywhere – on the swings, sitting on the swing frames, all over the climbing frame – and all of them were yelling, the kind of shouting that you hear at a football match.

'It's started,' said Brew.

Our group stopped and Meg spoke.

'OK. This is it. We all know what to do?'

Everyone nodded. Everyone except me. I had no idea what to do. I knew what I felt like doing but I didn't think that running away was on the agenda. Brew squeezed my hand.

'You stick beside me, Tills. We're not planning to get hurt. Last thing I want is to end up back in hospital. But if it looks like things aren't going our way just get out of here, OK?'

I nodded. No problemo. You wouldn't need to tell me twice.

'Everything's in place,' said Scar.

'Great,' said Brew. 'Well, let's do it then. Come on.'

Instead of continuing down the path, Brew led us off to the left. The grass was a bit damp and it was dark but I could see that we were still heading in the direction of the play park. Nobody said to keep quiet but it seemed obvious. We were moving slowly, trying not to be seen.

'Here,' whispered Brew. 'Put this on.'

It was a bandana and I didn't know what he meant. Put it on, how? And why? But I didn't need to ask because Meg, Scar and Brew were all covering their noses and mouths with the scarves and putting up their hoods. I tied my scarf on as well and we continued to creep over the grass. At the side of the park there was a concrete hut and we stopped when we got behind it. The noise was loud now. You could hear what the kids were shouting.

'Give it to her – the wee bitch!'

'Come on, Katrina – stick the boot in!'

And some of them weren't shouting words; they were just making noise, cheering and jeering, and the two fighters were shrieking at one another. The anger was enormous, like an animal. My whole body wanted to bolt. What could four people possibly do to stop something so out of control?

Meg was digging around in a bin liner that had been hidden by some twigs and leaves behind the hut. She pulled out a small CD player. Scar was moving more leaves and twigs around on the ground to reveal a long black shape.

'Thank God it's still here,' said Brew, stepping forward to retrieve the item. A guitar case.

'OK, help us up, then?'

Scar cupped his hands and Brew placed a foot into them and reached up for the top of the shed.

'Nearly. Try again.'

This time he made it. He lay down on the roof and held out an arm. Someone passed up the guitar and CD player. Next it was Meg's turn to get up. She placed a delicate boot into Scar's hands.

Two of them up. Scar nodded to me. I shook my head.

'You go up next – I'll get up on my own,' I whispered.

'Don't be daft – here.' He offered his cupped hands.

'And how will you get up, then?' I whispered.

He shrugged.

'Scar, let her go last,' said Brew. 'She's a climber, she can do it.'

I cupped my hands and smiled at Scar.

'Hope I don't hurt you!' he said.

He was heavy and I almost stumbled, but it was just for a moment. Brew and Meg hoisted him up and then it was just me. I could have bolted then. The voices on the other side had merged into a roar. I took a couple of breaths, trying to gather the impulse to run and channel it into my feet, my knees, my chest. There were a couple of chinks in the concrete where it had worn away. If I was fast enough, and strong enough, I could make it.

'Brew – and someone else – hold out your hands. I'm going to try and take a run at this.'

Brew and Scar leant out, their arms reaching towards me. I took a few steps back, paused and ran forward. I slammed myself into the wall and pushed up. My foot hit a chink in the concrete and I launched myself towards the top. Scar and Brew grabbed me and pulled me up. And then we were all on top of the concrete hut, crouched down at the edge of the park, behind all the kids on the play equipment who were yelling into the crowd, watching the savage war being waged between two young girls.

They were both on the ground, wrestling in the sand pit. It was hard to tell what was happening exactly but one had a fist of the other girl's hair and the other was kicking and yelling and both of them were hitting with hands and feet while a crowd of about fifty clapped and cheered.

I was so engrossed in the fight scene that I, along with those directly in front of us at the top of the climbing frame, turned around when the music started to find out what on earth was going on. Meg adjusted the volume on the CD player.

At first the music couldn't be heard over the shouting but after the first few people heard it the silence moved over the crowd like a Mexican wave and soon everyone was looking at the four of us on top of the concrete hut. Only the two girls, embroiled in battle, had not been distracted.

'The fuck is that?' said one of the kids on the swings.

It was circus music. The kind which makes you think of clowns tumbling out of a brightly coloured car and falling over one another as they run around in chaos.

'Here! Who are you? Fuck off!' yelled another kid.

The fighting girls realised that something had happened and they fell apart and stared at us, sitting on the hut, with the crappy little CD player playing this weird little tune.

One boy started trying to climb up the hut to get to us but he fell backwards, landing with a thud on his back.

'Are you all right, love?' said Meg with genuine concern.

'What the . . . ? Fuck *off!*' he shouted.

Meg shrugged and turned up the volume on the circus music. Nobody quite knew what to do. The girls were sitting on the edge of the sand pit now. One was holding her sleeve to her bloody nose. Both too exhausted to resume the fight.

When the song finished, Scar stood up and removed his bandana and addressed the crowd.

'We come in peace!'

'Faaaack off!' they shouted.

'Piss off, you fat freak!' one yelled.

Scar raised a pierced eyebrow and continued his address.

'We're not here to cause trouble. Just to say that we think it's brilliant that you've been so organised . . . '

*What?* I thought. *What about being a lover, not a fighter?*

'You know . . . youse could do really cool stuff if you organised yourselves like this more often,' he continued.

More cries of 'Fuck off, fatty.'

A boy with a shaved head stepped forward from one of the swings. He was wearing a bomber jacket and big laced-up boots. He walked right up to the bottom of the hut and, fists clenched, looked up at Scar towering above him.

'How about youse come down here, then?' he said.

The crowd, including both girls, yelled their support.

'Or, maybe, we should come up and see you?' He looked around and a few of his mates walked over to join him. None of them looked like they had come in peace. Meg took off her bandana and spoke.

'I'm a pensioner. We are no threat to you.' She clicked off the CD. 'We simply want to let you know that we admire your organisational skills.'

'Are youse cops or what?' said one of Bomber Jacket's friends.

'Nope,' said Brew, removing his scarf. 'We're just ordinary average freaks.'

'Yer takin' the piss, mate,' said Bomber Jacket. 'You're fuckin' up our buzz. And we're nat fuckin' happy about it. Are we, lawds?'

The 'lawds' shook their heads. The girls who had been fighting were still sitting on the edge of the sand pit, nursing their bruises. It didn't look as if we'd ruined *their* night.

'OK, look,' said Brew. 'We'll piss off. Just let us do one thing?'

'Oh aye, what's that?'

Brew reached down and picked up his guitar.

'I want to sing a song.'

'Whaaaat?' Bomber Jacket and the lads howled with

laughter. 'What are you?' he said. 'Some kind of gaylord? Fuck away off!'

'I'm a bit of a gaylord, in a way.' Brew winked at me. 'But just let me do this, and we'll clear off, I promise, and that'll be it – youse can go back to fighting or doing whatever.'

Bomber Jacket looked at his mates. One or two of them shrugged.

'Well, this'll be pure class. What's your wee gay song going to be about, you fruit?'

I caught Scar rolling his eyes and felt glad that Bomber Jacket hadn't noticed. The whole park was transfixed. Brew didn't answer; he played a chord, adjusted the tuning slightly, and began to play. The chord progression was simple but he played it fast, beating the rhythm of the song in perfect time.

> *Take a look at the man*
> *The man that built a war out of lies*
> *Take a look at the boy that's got everything*
> *The only thing he wants is suicide.*

As he sang, some of the kids laughed and shouted 'Yeooooo, faggot!' or 'Go on, Bob fuckin' Dylan!' but he closed his eyes. He was in the song and spitting out the lyrics like one of those angry preachers in the centre of town on a Saturday.

> *And the people in between get left behind*
> *And the people in between get left to die*
> *And the people get up in the morning*
> *Rocking the city with a hollow cry.*

Some of the other kids were cheering and clapping and although they meant to sound like they were mocking Brew, I couldn't help wondering if they were half enjoying it. Bomber Jacket and his mates were dancing around like idiots pretending they were at a rave. The sand pit girls were silent and watching it all closely.

> *And that's why*
> *We opened our eyes*
> *To the little white lies*
> *When you're looking for the bully*
> *You don't pick on the boy with the black eye.*

When he had finished, the crowd yelled and applauded and Bomber Jacket and his mates called for more, laughing their heads off. Brew opened his eyes and took a breath. Meg and Scar and I applauded too. Meg had tears in her eyes.

'Uh oh,' said Scar.

I looked to where his eyes were directed. The unmistakable shape of a group of police hats was moving towards the park in the shallow distance. Brew had seen it too.

'Scarves up!' he yelled to us. Turning to the crowd, he shouted, 'Thanks – it's been a blast. Make love, not war! And youse'd better split – the cops are on their way.'

Nobody needed to be told twice. Kids were jumping over walls and a few tried to run out the front entrance to the park as the cops were coming in. I reckoned they'd all just about made it but we were occupied with getting down off the hut ourselves without breaking any ankles or musical equipment.

We helped one another down, Meg shoved the CD player into the bin liner and Brew jammed his guitar into its case, and we were off, dragging one another by the hands into the darkest parts of the park until we knew we were safe.

# Organised Teen Brawl
# Disrupted by Police

# Chapter 31

Dad shook out the paper and tutted, crossing his legs.

'Listen to this, Tilly. This'll be that gang of thugs you used to hang round with, no doubt.'

I froze at the toaster. Oh God, no. Not again. Surely the cops didn't get a picture this time? We were well away by the time they'd reached the park. Maybe. But we had our scarves up, didn't we? I felt my shoulders loosen with the memory. There's no way anyone would have recognised me from a distance. I buttered the hot toast. Dad continued.

'It says here that they organised a massive brawl in the park last night. Hundreds of youths, apparently! Organised on social media!'

Hundreds of youths? Hardly. I mean, it was big enough – why did they have to exaggerate it? I was curious now. I sat down at the table opposite Dad as he read aloud from the article.

'. . . the gang of unknowns were seen dancing and singing on top of a concrete shelter, leading the crowd, who were shouting and jeering at the fighters ... police think it was the same group who have been involved in other disturbances of the peace lately.'

What? How did the cops even know there was a fight? It was over before they got there!

'... a local woman described the scene: "I was just out walking my dog when I heard them shouting at one another. The language was just dreadful and it was two wee girls tearing lumps out of one another. You wouldn't think that could happen in our wee park, would you? Young girls!"'

Dad lowered his paper and looked at me over the top of it.

'Are you glad now? That you're well away from them? You can see the trouble they get into. They'll end up on the dole, or worse – in prison! Bunch of louts, Tilly.'

He raised his paper before I could answer. I finished my toast and left without saying anything. On one hand, I was enraged that the paper had got it so wrong. They had put two stories together – the woman walking her dog's story and the police's story – and they'd made the whole thing look like it was my friends' fault. They knew they could get away with it, because who was going to argue? Meg was hardly going to phone them up and say, 'Look here old bean, I'm simply the wealthiest person you've ever met and I'm one of those "unknowns", I'll have you know ...'

But on the other hand, I was glad. Because Dad obviously really believed that I wasn't involved with them any more. And the more wrong he was about them, the better it was for me. The rush of relief gave way to a pang of guilt. Not just because Dad trusted me, but because I knew that the reason he needed to believe that I was being well-behaved was because he was always so worried about doing it right – about being a Good Dad. That's why school was important to him. And all the clubs he had made me go to as a kid – hockey, drama, choir . . . everything that I eventually wriggled out of by convincing him that I was going to be fine without constant attention. Without two parents. I had learnt to play the role so well, and he wanted to believe it so badly, that I found it easy to start sneaking out to do what I wanted to do. The play park graffiti incident? He had already decided that that was a teenage mistake and that I had learnt my lesson. And as long as he couldn't picture his dear daughter with a dangerous gang who organised fights and terrorised the city, he wasn't going to go snooping around to find out where I really was.

Beth, on the other hand, knew exactly who the news article was about and she was on the phone about ten minutes after I'd left the kitchen.

'Oh my God, Tilly, were you there? Why did they organise that fight? Did anyone get really mashed?'

It didn't take long to fill her in on the truth of the situation but she wasn't really much happier about it.

'Relax,' I said, 'Dad has no idea, and actually it turned into a really cool night, and no, nobody got seriously mashed – we broke it up before that happened.'

'Wow, you really are heroes, aren't you?'

She was being sarcastic but I imagined a hint of actual admiration in her voice. Because yeah, they were heroes. Not me, really – I was just there, watching – but I had felt closer than ever to the action, like I could have joined in, like next time maybe I would be a hero too. And so what if it was a silly thing, like singing a song in order to ruin a fight? It was something. It was brave. Just thinking about Brew standing up there, eyes shut, ignoring the lads shouting at him and getting into the song like he really believed it would make something good happen ... I wanted to be like him, to be free like that. I wondered how many of the kids watching him last night felt like that too. Maybe it would never happen, but who knew? Maybe next time they'd be heroes too.

'Earth to Tilly?' said Beth.

'Eh?'

'I asked you about the history assignment?'

'Oh. Right. I'll talk to you in school about it later. Better go and get a shower,' I said.

To be honest, I had no idea which history assignment she meant.

# Chapter 32

Saturday morning. I used to sleep in, but now I didn't even need an alarm to wake me early. For a couple of weeks everything seemed perfect. Saturday was the day when I could hang out at the courthouse all day. If I got there early I had breakfast with them. Apparently, Meg lived the farthest away so she might have stayed from the night before. I hated missing Friday nights but the less risk of Dad finding out that I'd been with them regularly, the better, so I always left early. I knew that at the squat on a Friday night they'd sit into the wee small hours drinking Brew's beer and singing and telling ridiculously cheesy ghost stories, or going over old missions.

That was my favourite thing – hearing about what they'd been up before I knew them. Sara, sitting cross-legged and looking tiny beside Scar, told me about the time her dad almost caught her climbing out the window to meet everyone.

'I was half out of the room, head first. Dad walked in to be greeted by my bum wiggling in the window frame. I had to tell him I was trying to rescue a pigeon that had got stuck with its beak in the bird feeder outside my window and had just managed to free it before he came in.'

'Tell me he didn't believe that!' said Scar.

'I'm sure he didn't,' laughed Sara, taking a sip of her beer. 'But what could he do? He's never caught me and I've never made him in the least bit suspicious.' She smiled proudly. 'He thinks I'm the best daughter ever. I don't smoke, or drink' – she pretended to hide the bottle with a giggle – 'and I don't have boyfriends . . .'

Meg laughed. 'And what about the girlfriends?' she said.

Sara made a face. 'Ssssh, he might hear you!'

Everyone laughed then. Sara's stories about her dad's strict set of rules were legendary. No drinking, smoking, drugs, obviously. But also no TV after 8 p.m., and only channels he approved, none of that 'American degenerate crap'. No boys, no rock music, no biker boots . . .

'The thing about Daddy is,' Sara said, 'he's so uptight that he hasn't even considered the things I might *want* to get up to.'

She winked at Meg and took another drink.

I knew what she meant. Up until Dad saw my picture in the paper it would never have even crossed his mind that his daughter might want to be out late at night with a group of people taking the law into their own hands. Those kinds of people were not 'our' people. Those kinds of people – the others, the ones who crossed lines and spray-painted parks and turned up at organised fights – were dangerous and weird, an anomaly, the kind of people Dad wrote about, not the kind of people he wanted me to associate with.

166

I thought about it as I crossed the road that Saturday morning towards the old courthouse. He hadn't even asked where I was going this morning. That was the sign that everything was 100 per cent OK. He was assuming that I was going to the library or into town.

When I got to the squat, Brew was hoovering. And singing. Loudly. I stood in the doorway for a couple of minutes watching him going over the floor and giving his performance everything he had, like he was playing the end of tour gig at Wembley stadium. When I finally caught his eye, he broke into a huge grin but he didn't stop singing. He clicked off the hoover and finished the song, using the hose as a mic.

'How long you been standing there, then?' he asked when he had finished.

'Long enough, Lady Gaga.'

He came over and put his hands on my hips.

'Is Lady Gaga a lesbian?' he asked.

My arms circled his neck.

'No idea,' I said.

'Let's say she is,' he said. 'And then I can be her and still do this.'

We kissed for longer than before. His mouth, warm and soft, our arms around one another. How to make a disused, broken-down building feel like the most luxurious space on earth.

'Does this make me a lesbian too?' I asked, my forehead against his.

'I suppose if I'm a female pop legend we can still be bi,' he said.

'As long as you know that I only want you, Lady Gaga.'

We kissed again, resting against the door frame, locked into one another like a completed jigsaw. When we finally took a breath, we didn't speak. My head was on his shoulder. His arms traced my spine. We stood like that for a while. Maybe a minute. Maybe ten minutes.

Meg was suddenly there. She must have walked the length of the hall to get to us but we both jumped to hear her voice.

'Good morning, lovebirds!'

We broke apart and Brew straightened out his shirt.

'Hi, Meg. What's happened to your hands?'

They were black, covered in what looked like car oil.

'I've been working with the Rats, love. Just off to get a towel. Brew will fill you in.'

She kissed me on both cheeks, both hands raised in the air so that they didn't touch me, and went off in the direction of the makeshift kitchen/brewing room.

'Rats?'

It sounded familiar.

Brew moved back to the hoover.

'Just let me get this put away and I'll tell you all about it.'

I watched him wind the hoover's flex carefully around its body, unplug it from the adapter that stretched from the generator, and wheel it into the corner.

'Never had you down as Mrs Mop,' I said.

'Hey,' he said, fake-punching me on the arm. 'The revolution doesn't have to look like a shithole, you know. We all do our bit.'

He was right. When I thought back to the party I

remembered black bin bags everywhere, and even the scariest-looking people dutifully putting their empties into them. I thought about the kids in my class at school and how we'd once left a school bus looking so trashed that the driver, who only noticed the mess when he got to the depot, had driven it the whole way back to our school and insisted that the head make us get on board and clean it up. We argued for ages over that – who was on the bus, who had made the most mess, who was going to lift the half-chewed Refreshers bars, who was going to mop up the lemonade . . . Everything about Brew and his mates made school seem like a toddlers' playgroup.

We slumped down on the big bean bag and ruched it around us until it was comfortable. It was a bright day outside, but the inside of the squat was mostly dark. The windows had been boarded up and the odd shaft of light pierced through like a miniature spotlight on the concrete floor. I liked it. I heard that in Las Vegas in the casinos they took away all the clocks and blacked out the windows so that nobody could tell if it was night or day. People would stay up all night gambling without realising it. Who invented hours, anyway? If you take away all the words and all the light then there would be no such thing as time. Just me and Brew and everything between us and around us.

His fingers curled around mine and we sat in the quiet and kissed for a minute before Brew said, 'Right. Coffee? I need a coffee.'

'Yeah, OK. Ta. And then you can tell me about Meg and the rats?'

He laughed. 'Yeah. Back in a sec.'

I stretched out on the bean bag and checked my phone. Text from Beth asking about some assignment or other. I put the phone back in my pocket and wished I hadn't checked it. I could smell the coffee before Brew entered the room. He didn't have much to his name – his guitar, his brewing equipment and a backpack with a few pens and notebooks. But he always had the best coffee. He told me that Meg had bought him an AeroPress for Christmas, and a voucher for S. D. Bell's. I knew that place because my granny always bought people tea from S. D. Bell's at Christmas time. You could tell that this coffee was good stuff. Rich and strong and smooth. *Why doesn't everyone live like this*, I thought, *with only the things they really needed?*

Brew set the tray on the floor and sat down on a bean bag opposite mine.

'Oooh, cake!'

'Yeah, Meg made it. You've not had cake until you've had Meg's Victoria sponge.'

*Maybe her servants made it*, I thought, and then I scolded myself for being a bitch. Meg was always so kind – so what if she was loaded? It felt weird, though, knowing who she was and not talking about it with her. How could you ever bring it up? *Hey, Meg, guess what? I know you're a bazillionaire who lives in a mansion.*

I took a bite of cake.

'Oh my God.'

'I know, isn't it amazing?'

It is no exaggeration to say that I never knew cake could taste so good. The sponge was like velvety clouds of vanilla and the heavy cream filling kept it from floating out of my mouth.

'This,' I said, with my mouth full of cake, 'is the sexiest cake known to man or woman.'

'It is sex personified,' agreed Brew.

I wondered if Brew had ever had sex. Maybe I should have asked him how he knew what sex personified was like? But I was scared of the answer. What if the answer was, 'Er, because I've had sex loads of times?' and then I'd feel like one of the toddlers in my class at school again ...

It was great cake, though, and I waited until it was gone before bringing up Meg's rats.

'So, OK,' I said. 'Rats?'

'Rat bikes. You remember?'

Of course – the bikers at the party who made their own bikes. But, hang on ...

'Meg's a biker?'

Brew choked on his cake.

'No! Hahaha! Can you imagine her zooming down the M1 in her shoulder pads on a Harley?'

Actually, I reckoned I could. Meg was the most surprising person I had ever met.

'Well ... what's she doing with the bikers, then?'

'The Rats are helping us, with the big plan. They're out back now fixing up the bikes for a wee recce later.'

The big plan. The Maze prison plan. I hadn't thought about it since he told me that night at the cafe.

'You're still doing that, then?'

He raised an eyebrow.

'Of course. Why wouldn't we be?'

'I just thought ... well, after the fight at the park and all, and how it ended up in the paper and stuff . . . like, maybe you'd be lying low for a bit?'

I hadn't thought that; I'd hoped it. Lying low was really not Brew's thing. But the Maze prison – it seemed like a crazy idea. And yet, there was part of me that thrilled to hear how casually he considered the danger of it.

'Nah! The park was great! Didn't you think it was great? We totally rocked!'

He sat up straight and put down his coffee cup.

'You have to learn to ignore the papers – they're always going to be pushing a right-wing agenda. They hate us, and we don't care!' His eyes lit up and he pointed his finger at some invisible listener just out of my eyeline. 'They're sad bastards with nothing else to do in their sad lives but have a go at young people, or poor people, or whoever it is they can't stand that week. And it'll always be someone – I like to think we're saving some other fecker from a going-over if it's us in the headlines.'

Oh God. I would have to tell him about Dad some day. Not now, though . . . not yet. I nodded, wishing I hadn't brought the park fight up. I *had* enjoyed it. But I wondered if it had really changed anything for those kids?

Brew was still animated, now up on his feet and searching through his coat pocket.

'Here,' he said. 'Look at this!'

He handed me the phone. It was a screen grab showing the news feed from the social media account he'd shown me on the night of the fight.

'I saved it yesterday when I had some Wi-Fi at the cafe.'

I recognised some of the names but the hashtag had changed, to #BELNINJA1.

> @NinjaB223 to @janetison East side of park. 10.30. BYOM. Pass it on. #BELNINJA1
>
> @janetison The fk is BYOM?I'll be there with Bucky! #BELNINJA1
>
> @NinjaB223 @janetison Bring yer own music? #BELNINJA1
>
> @janetison @NinjaB223 Dead on. Ed Sheeran an da Buckeeeee! #BELNINJA1
>
> @weejonny735 I'll be der. Two rules: everyone gets to play their thing. Everyone dances. #BELNINJA1
>
> @offmahead Long as everyone's drinkin sounds good to me! #BELNINJA1
>
> @janetison Pass it on till everyone you know. The more ppl the better. #BELNINJA1

'What is this?' I handed the phone back to Brew.

'It is' – he put the phone back his pocket, grinning widely – 'Belfast's very first ninja gig cooperative.'

'Eh? What's a ninja gig?'

I poured myself another coffee – just warm enough. Brew did the same and he sat down again opposite me.

'It's a thing Amanda Palmer invented. You know Amanda Palmer, right?'

I nodded. Amanda Palmer, the punk singer. I'd seen some of her videos on YouTube.

'Well,' he went on, 'she organises these gigs online. In places like parks or town squares. It's free and unofficial and ...'

'Illegal?'

'Maybe sometimes . . . They're organised online, at the last minute.'

'Like the fight.'

'Exactly. Only this is something so much cooler.'

'But how did that lot go from thinking that we were the biggest bunch of losers they ever saw, to wanting to do it for themselves?'

Brew grinned. 'Come on. We had a great time, didn't we?'

'Well, yeah, but *they* thought we were dicks.'

'We *all* had a great time! That overrides everything. Everyone wants to have a bit of craic. *They* had a great time making fun of us. Far more fun than they had watching two girls batin' the heads of each other.'

'I guess . . . '

Brew shrugged. 'I guess they'll see when they get there. Maybe old NinjaB223 knew what he was talking about, maybe not . . . '

'Oh, wait.' I put down my coffee. 'Are *you* NinjaB?'

He laughed. 'Yep.'

'And are you going? To the ninja gig?'

'Nah. They're on their own. They'll be grand – they have each other. And you saw how that Jonny guy was starting to talk about rules and stuff. I reckon they'll have a good night, have a drink and a dance, and they'll still get a chase from the peelers. This time nobody'll end up in A&E, though. You finished with that coffee?'

He got up and took my empty cup and the other stuff back to the kitchen. It was a different life. Caring about kids you didn't know, who were beating each other up, but not bothering if it was your own face getting mashed. I didn't know anyone else like him. I couldn't decide if he was brave or reckless and I wondered if there was much difference between the two. Somehow with Brew you never had time to wonder about it for too long, because there was always something else to do – always another action, always so fast that you had to trust your instincts.

That's what it felt like when he returned and took my hand and led me outside. The sun was blinding after being in the darkness and there were three enormous bikes in front of us. All of them were dull grey. A silver skull with a pirate patch over one eye was stuck on the front of one, like the figure on the front of a ship looking out. Two of the bikes had two wheels and one had three, but all of them seemed twice as big as regular motorcycles. One had a black and red flag attached to the pillion seat. Meg was standing in between a large bearded man and a tall woman with red hair, both in overalls, and another of the Rats was revving the engine on the trike. His tattooed arms bulged out of a sleeveless denim jacket and when he revved the engine the big chains around his wrists jangled together.

'Aye, this one's good to go,' he yelled over the noise. 'That's the lot of them, Meg!'

Meg clapped her hands in delight and then cupped them around the face of the Rat on the trike and kissed him loudly on the cheek. The other two bikers cheered and the Rat on the trike looked sheepish.

'Well!' said Meg, when the engine had died down. 'I think

we'll all have a nice cup of tea and then set off, shall we? Are you joining us, Tilly? I do hope so, darling!'

Meg skipped back into the building, followed by the three bikers, who squeezed their leather-bound bodies through the little window, leaving Brew and me outside with the bikes. Brew patted the pirate skull on the head.

'You can borrow one of my jackets if you like. It'll be cold on the bikes.'

He had assumed I was going. But there was no point in arguing with him – I knew I was going too. I had planned to spend all day with Brew and that's what I was going to do. Dad would go spare if he knew. I doubted that whether I was in a derelict building in Belfast or a derelict building in Lisburn would make any difference. And that's how I ended up with my arm around a biker called Big George, tearing down the M1 on a massive motortrike, on our way to break in to a prison.

# Chapter 33

It was different than I had expected. The main gates were easy to clear – only about ten feet high or so. Meg applauded as I scaled them and dropped down the other side, looking for a way in for the bikes. In the end it was easy – there was a catch on the inside that opened a smaller gate, which was built into the big one. Two of the bikes got through with no problem and we heaved the trike in on its side. It was like the time Dad and I tried to move the sofa from the living room into the kitchen: two doors and a hallway and neither of us could see the other person, and once we got it into the kitchen Dad decided it was too big and we had to bring it back out again. So we lumbered around with the trike until we got it through. Big George smiled in relief as he dusted it off and started the engine up again.

'That's my girl,' he said to the trike.

Brew smirked at me.

We got onto the bikes again and rode to the nearest building which was at the end of a completely straight road. The further we got from the main road, the stranger it became. When the bikes stopped, everyone got off and looked around in silence. The expanse was huge and still and quiet. I pulled Brew's heavy coat around me. It couldn't have been any colder here than it had been five minutes ago at the entrance to the prison, but I could see Meg rubbing her hands together too. The wide, open space was surrounded by concrete buildings. To the left there were several long tin huts with curved roofs, like a series of pipes cut lengthwise. To the right and further away there were a couple of huge buildings.

'Are those the H-Blocks?' I said.

'Yes,' said Meg. 'Right,' she said, looking at me, 'you and Brew check the huts and I'll head over there with George. OK, George?'

He nodded and indicated the pillion seat of his trike to Meg.

'Meet you back here in an hour?'

'No worries,' said Brew, and Meg and Big George sped off with Meg's hair blowing in the freezing air.

I giggled.

'What's so funny?' He nudged me as we walked towards the huts.

'Meg,' I said.

'She's one of a kind,' he said.

'Brew. I know about her.'

'What do you mean?'

The sun was shining, Brew and I were alone in a strange place, about to discover who knows what, and nobody knew we were here, and it didn't frighten me because I had crossed the line that maybe everyone in the gang crosses at some point – the line of possibility, where fear becomes wonder and all you can think of is what's next. It was a good time to ask him about stuff. I knew I was in. I knew it was safe to ask. We reached the door of the first hut but I stopped and took Brew's hand before we went any further. He turned towards me and the sun on his face made it seem golden.

'Meg. She's, like, aristocracy or something.'

Brew took my other hand as well. He kissed both hands, one at a time, before answering.

'Not quite. But she's rich.'

'We saw a film in school. She was in it. At her house. It's like, this huge mansion.'

'I know.'

'Well, I mean, what's she doing here, going round with people on big dirty bikes called Rats and hanging out with . . .' I paused.

'With poor people?'

*Yes, with poor people, I thought. With people who live in a squat. With people who get involved in riots. People who don't seem to have that much to lose . . .*

But I didn't answer him because he knew that's what I meant and it seemed wrong to point it out.

'Sometimes,' I said, 'I feel like I don't know you lot very well at all.'

Brew looked up at the sky and sighed loudly, dropping my hands.

'Well, ask then,' he said. 'If you wanna know something, fuck sake, ask.'

'Don't be cross,' I said. But it was too late.

'You know more about me than I know about you,' he said, looking me in the eyes again.

'That's not true. I hardly know . . . '

'You've seen my life story art – hardly anyone sees that. You know where I live – hardly anyone knows that. You've seen me in hospital, you know about my family, you know who my friends are, you've had beer that I made at my place . . . What else do you want to know? That Meg sometimes pays for my guitar strings? There isn't anything else. That's all there is to me, Tilly. That's literally all there is.'

His eye glistened and I looked down at the ground. I wished I hadn't started it. I thought of everything he hadn't said. That he'd never been at my house. That he'd never met my dad. That he had no idea who my family were or what they might do if they knew where I was right now and who with . . .

'I'm sorry,' I whispered.

I felt his hand in mine again.

'Come on,' he said, giving it a squeeze. 'Let's have a look at this auld place.'

'Wait.' I tugged his arm to make him stop again. 'Listen. I'm going to tell you a thing. Something I should've told you ages ago.'

And so I told him about Dad and about how it was his paper that kept on writing articles about the 'gang of unknowns' who were terrorising the city, and about how he'd be beyond insanely angry if he found out about my involvement with Brew, and how he'd call the cops for absolutely definite if he knew about the squat and the parties. And I knew it was a risk, me telling him, but I knew you can't be free without taking risks and it was Brew who taught me that, so I owed him the truth.

When I had finished he said, 'Forty-five minutes.'

'What?'

'That's all we've got left and we haven't even gotten inside yet.' He nodded at the tin hut behind us.

'Is that it? You're not going to say anything?' I could feel my eyes filling up.

'C'mere,' he said.

He put his arms around me and I slotted mine through the gaps and around his back.

'I'm not afraid of your dad, Tilly,' he whispered without breaking free, 'and you're not afraid of him either – otherwise you wouldn't be here.' He released his hold and I did too. 'OK?' He kissed my head.

I nodded. We began walking towards the hut, hand in hand. 'Everyone's got people who want to hold them back,' he said. 'You have to find your own way. Otherwise you're living their life and not your own.' He stopped walking and turned to face me. 'Do I sound like a dick?'

'What?' I burst out laughing.

'I just heard myself there. I sound like one of those self-help dicks.' He made a peace sign with both hands. 'Ooooh, love and peace, man, just follow your destineeeee.'

'Haha! Come on then, dickhead, only forty minutes now.'

The door to the hut was locked but Brew picked it easily with his pocket knife.

Inside it was freezing. The cold air clung to us and our breath spilled out in clouds. There was a long corridor with rooms, dormitories off each side of it and a large kitchen at the end.

'Do you think prisoners stayed in here?' I said. 'It doesn't look much like an actual prison.'

'I don't think it,' he said, flicking an electric switch to no avail, 'I know it.' He clicked a torch and we looked around the murky room. A line of beds, maybe six or so. No mattresses. A sink beside each bed and a high shelf above each sink. And that was all. 'My great uncle was in one of these.'

'Wow! What did he do?'

As soon as I asked it I wasn't sure that I really wanted to know.

'Not much. Gun running.' Brew was peering into the sinks and tracing the light around the walls but there was nothing else to see. 'They found a load of guns in his shed. He never properly joined up but he helped them out when they needed it. You kind of had to. And then he got caught on and ended up here.'

'But, if he had to . . . like, if they forced him . . . ?'

'Well, he wasn't gonna tout on them, was he?'

I supposed not. I'd never met anyone whose family was in jail before, but I knew a bit about the Troubles from stories people told in school, mostly about relatives who died or got injured in bomb attacks. But everyone knew what happened to touts, whether they'd been forced into helping or not. I tried to change the subject.

'So, what exactly are we looking for here?'

'What? Oh, just whatever, really . . . ' We were out into the corridor and into the next dorm – just the same as the one before.

'Soooo, what's the plan?'

'The plan?' His torchlight sent a spotlight around the room. You could half see everything anyway, but the torch helped a bit. The windows were small and high and most of the light that got in was trapped near the dome of the ceiling.

'Yeah, the plan? What are we doing here exactly?'

'Oh,' said Brew, clicking off the torch and facing me again. 'We haven't sorted out the details yet. Here.'

Brew took a can of spray paint from his pocket and threw it over to me.

'What's this?'

'Shake it up! It's a rattle can. You used one before?'

I shook my head.

'There's a bit of a knack to it, but you'll soon get it.'

I stared at the tin.

'Is this the plan? Is this where we're going to do it? These walls?'

Brew shrugged. 'Up to you.'

'Well, what do I write?'

He grinned and did the same shrug. It was up to me.

I chucked the can back to him. 'I can't. It's not right. It's not the same as painting over someone else's bad graffiti, is it? If I just write on a clean wall it's like proper vandalism, isn't it?'

Brew put the can back into his jacket pocket, not showing any sign of disappointment. 'I guess it depends what you put on the wall,' he said.

*Maybe*, I thought. But what could I put on a wall that would make it OK to write on a wall?

'It's someone else's wall,' I said.

'Is it?' he replied.

He wandered out into the corridor again. We had scoped the extent of the hut. Not much to see – plenty of bare walls, if that's what the Big Plan was. But there were plenty of bare walls in Belfast too. Why had we come all the way out here to find a derelict building? We made our way towards the outside again and I thought about the inmates who had lived here. All men. Some of them killers, probably. It made me shiver. Or maybe it was just the cold.

'What do you mean "is it?"' I said. 'It's not my place – I know that much.'

'The courthouse isn't mine either,' he said.

'Oh, I didn't mean . . . I mean, your mural is really good – it's, like, art, and if I wrote something on a wall it'd just be, like . . . crap.'

In the distance we could see Meg and Big George approaching on the Rat bike.

'Tilly,' said Brew, grabbing my hand tightly so that I caught my breath. He looked utterly serious. 'Nothing about you is crap. Nothing.'

'Oh, uh, thanks,' I said.

'No.' He squeezed my hand harder. 'Seriously. Don't say shit like that – you'll end up believing it.'

'OK, thanks, Oprah.' I tried to smile at him but he wasn't going to let me lighten the mood and we stood there quietly until Meg and George reached us.

Meg removed her helmet. She was breathless.

'You have to come and see this!' She beamed.

# Chapter 34

Once we were all gathered together, the Rats took us to where Meg had been. 'This' turned out to be one of the H-Blocks. Meg and Big George had fiddled the locks to the entrance and found their way to what seemed to be a control room. A large desk faced a wall of old television screens. A filing cabinet stood in the corner like a grey monument to law and order. Everything neat and tidy, even though it hadn't been touched in years.

'Just imagine!' said Meg. 'All those people being watched. Their every move, every day.'

She made it sound like they were sad laboratory puppies being bred for experiments. I didn't say anything, though. Who knows what her family had been through. That's one thing that everyone here agrees on about the Troubles – nobody was safe. Sure if you lived in a rough area you were more in danger, but having a load of money didn't mean you'd never be unlucky. And Meg was probably related to royalty in some way. She'd've been someone's target for sure. She was sitting on the desk, looking at the dark screens as if she could see back into the past. I wondered if she was looking for anyone in particular.

Snapping out of her trance, she suddenly turned to Brew.

'Come on, let's go and see the rooms. The cells, I mean.'

The internal gates were unlocked and she and George led us through them and up the clanging metal stairs, along the narrow platforms that looked out over a dark rectangular floor. Then we were in a corridor, with damp walls and doors along one side.

'This is it,' whispered Meg, as if the ghosts of the prisoners could hear her. She stopped outside one of the doors.

'This is what?' said Brew.

Meg opened the door slowly, as if she was revealing the answer to a great mystery. It was a very small room, just about the length of a person, and just about wide enough to contain a small metal bed frame with a space beside it for the prisoner to get in and out. It was nothing, really. Just a small room. We couldn't have fitted inside it, so we stood in the corridor and looked at it, waiting to see whatever it was that Meg had seen to make her so excited.

'So?' said Brew. 'What's the deal?'

Meg's shoulders dropped.

'It's his room! At least I think it is. I'm pretty sure that's how James described the location.'

'Whose room?' I said.

'Bobby Sands!' said Meg.

Bobby Sands. The IRA prisoner who had died on hunger strike. Dad told me once how he'd been stuck in Derry the day of Bobby Sands' funeral. The cortège was so enormous that the traffic didn't move for hours. Sands was a hero to a lot of people. But not people like Meg, normally. Not people with money. But I didn't say anything. Maybe I'd ask Brew later, I thought. Meg was in her trance again, staring at the dank little cell. It was staring to freak me out. I felt like getting Brew's rattle can and painting the walls a different colour. I was tired of grey and the coldness and the darkness.

'Imagine being stuck in here every day,' said Brew, as if he was thinking the same thing.

George looked at his phone.

'Folks, I've got to be home by five. We'll have to leave soon,' he said.

The rest of the tour took place quickly and without much chat. We walked through a few more corridors, down the stairs to the communal area, around the freezing outside, leaving our footprints in the gravel where the prisoners had taken exercise. And that was it. Since the cells Meg seemed more serious, but to be honest the place hadn't moved me. It was big. A big, empty building. It seemed sad, if anything. All those prisoners, all those lives, and had it made any difference? And now it was going to ruin – dirty plaster beginning to crumble, iron rusting. It would eventually get overgrown. I wondered if it would ever get forgotten, or if other people would move in, the way Brew had moved into the courthouse. Why not? Why not let people have it? But I knew why. We walked back to the bikes, crunching over the stony ground. Once there had been an idea to turn the prison into a peace centre, but our politicians couldn't agree on it. Some thought it would turn into a memorial for terrorism. So they decided to do nothing. To just let it sink instead. I could feel my heart starting to thump, the way it did on a climb. I knew we needed to go. But it would only take a minute.

'Brew,' I said, grabbing his arm, breathless.

'Yeah? What's up, you OK?'

'Yeah. Can I have the spray?' I said.

'Eh?'

'The rattle can. Just, quickly – can I have it?'

Brew grinned and reached inside his jacket. He handed me the can and I took off.

'Can I come?' he yelled, but I didn't answer – there was no time. He followed me anyway and I heard him yell to Meg and the others, 'Just a second! Won't be long!'

I got to the hut and shook the can hard. Now I knew. I knew what to write and I knew it was OK and I knew that this place was mine as much as anyone's. Brew stood, panting, with his arms folded as I set to work, writing in foot-high letters along the front of the hut, in purple spray.

FREE ALL THE PEOPLE! ULSTER BELONGS TO EVERYONE.

'Yeeeooooooow!' he yelled, clapping, as I finished off. 'Go on Tilly!'

It wasn't the world's greatest literature but my head was fizzing. I felt powerful.

I laughed and hugged Brew and we kissed and clung together for a moment. And then we were off again, running back to the bikes, the Rats and Meg. Everything was perfect.

# Sectarian Graffiti at
# Maze Prison Site

# Chapter 35

'I don't even know what I'm doing here. I'm not in the band.'

'Wise up. You're an essential member. And, by the way, you look totally hot in that dress,' said Scar.

We were in the biggest kitchen I'd ever seen in my life. It was seriously the size of our whole downstairs. Scar looked hot too, I had to admit. He was wearing a tuxedo with a coral pink dicky bow to match his nails and eyeshadow. Brew had a tux on too but his was all black. Both of them had brushed their hair. I think Scar had combed his beard as well. The three of us were sitting on the enormous table in the centre of the kitchen, Brew playing with the silver salt and pepper set, me dangling my high heels off my toes. Well, Meg's high heels. I had never worn high heels before. They weren't even very high but I knew I wouldn't have them on all night. I was uncomfortable enough in one of Meg's ballgowns. Earlier that evening she had laid a dozen of them on her bed, inviting me to try them on and choose one.

'Start with whichever takes your fancy, love. I have shoes to match them all.'

I picked up a blue sequined dress which gathered under the chest and floated out like the sea. It felt like something a mermaid would wear, heavy and shiny with scales that shimmered in the bright bulbs around Meg's dressing table.

'Oh, that one's my favourite too,' she said, touching the hem of the dress. 'A gift. From a Russian princess.'

I set it back down.

'Oh dear,' said Meg, picking it up again. 'Don't let that put you off!'

'But it must be so expensive. I'd probably spill something on it. And it wouldn't fit me anyway.'

Meg looked me up and down.

'Actually, I think it will. The top bit is more accommodating than it looks. And I hope you *will* spill something on it. This dress has not been worn enough. It deserves to have a good time.'

It was beautiful.

'Oh, Tilly!' said Meg as I walked into the bedroom from her changing room. 'You look absolutely divine!'

I felt my face flush. To be honest, I felt 'absolutely divine' as well. I would have never chosen something like this myself. I wondered how far I could climb in a dress like this. When she brought out the shoes to match I wondered if I'd even be able to walk across the room.

'Just think of it as a fancy-dress party. That's what I do,' said Meg.

I looked at myself in her full-length mirror. *This is me,*

*dressed as a rich person*, I thought. But with Meg it wasn't pretend – she *was* a rich person.

'It's different for you, though, Meg.'

She stood beside me, looking in the mirror, and put an arm around my shoulder.

'Yes, it is,' she sighed.

'Don't you like it?' I said.

'Don't I like what?'

'Being rich? Having all this amazing stuff. I mean, why . . . '

'You get used to it,' she said, plonking herself down on the bed as if she was wearing an old tracksuit. 'Being rich, I mean.' I let her continue, aware that we didn't have much time before she'd have to leave. 'Of course, it's nice when you don't have to worry about money,' Meg said, 'and you get the opportunity to do things like this – charity events which can raise huge amounts of cash. It's very exciting sometimes!' She paused and took a breath. There were portraits on the wall, all of fancy-looking women. It was like they were watching us. 'But it can be lonely as well,' Meg continued. 'I spent years feeling like an absolute freak, knowing that nobody knew what it was like to be me, related to all posh strangers' – she waved at the nosy women on the wall – 'but you can't really complain about it when you have maids to clean the bathroom and iron your knickers, can you?'

'Do they really . . . ?

'Yes, really! They're very thorough!'

Meg gave me a sideways look and we both giggled. She patted the bed beside her and I plonked myself down the same way she had done. She sighed deeply.

'I wanted some company – someone ... some *people* to be real with. I would sit and watch the news and feel ever so pissed off with the badness going on and I'd think, what can you do about it, Meg? You have all the cash you need and you can give to charity and start educational programmes and volunteer at food banks ... and I do all that ... but ... what can you really do?'

It sounded to me like she did a lot. Dad gave to charity sometimes. I mean, we weren't as rich as Meg, but he'd give a donation in the street sometimes if there was a collector with stickers and a tin. But he'd never give change to a homeless person. He suspected them all of being drug addicts or gangsters.

'I wanted to know who was doing things in their area without having all the cash,' said Meg. 'Who were the people who never get on the news? Who were the freaks who didn't care if people thought they were odd because they were just getting on with helping out. You know?'

I thought of Brew at the bottom of the gigantic crane. Offering me coffee. Saying he came over because he thought I might be about to jump. Most people don't go over and talk to strangers who they think might jump off a crane. Most people would just go home and hope they didn't hear about it on the news the next day.

'Yeah, I think I get it,' I said. 'How did you meet Brew and Scar, though?'

She smiled broadly, jumping up from the bed.

'Wait there!'

It was a couple of minutes before Meg came back into the room. Enough time for me to think about how much she must have trusted me, sitting here in her expensive clothes, with her jewellery lying around the room and even a couple of twenties casually lying on the dressing table. I was dying to hear how she met Brew but I also wondered how she became this person who didn't mind letting other people in – poor people. I didn't know anyone else like that.

'Here it is!' she sang as she entered the room again, waving a huge silver-fronted album.

She sat down beside me and flipped the pages until she'd found what she wanted to show me.

'There!' she said proudly.

It was a photo of Brew, a couple of years younger. He looked just the same. Maybe slightly skinnier, and his hair was longer, but same face, same smile. He was holding a guitar and standing outside Eason in the city centre.

'He was busking when you met?'

'He was. I was walking past on my way to the city hall for a long meeting with some terminally boring planning group, and I hadn't noticed him, to be honest. I was rushing and I was in a bad mood.'

'Because of the terminally boring planners?'

'Exactly. Good God, those committee meetings drag on like you would not believe. Anyway . . . '

Meg told me how she'd been rushing, thinking about the meeting, worrying about how it had started to rain and she wasn't wearing a coat. And then, 'I fell! Oh God, Tilly, it probably looked comical!' She covered her face, recalling the moment. 'My face actually hit the pavement.'

'Scundered!' I said.

'Exactly!' Meg laughed. 'I tried to get up but my ankle gave way under me. I yelped like a little puppy. And that's when your lovely Brew came to my rescue.'

Meg grinned and squeezed my arm. I could imagine him rushing over to help her up, leaving his precious guitar, knowing that anyone could just take it. Maybe it was Brew who had less reason to trust people. Meg could always buy more jewellery.

'He gallantly helped me over to a bench, took £1.50 out of his busking hat and instructed me to sit tight and watch his "gear". It was all such a blur that I didn't know what he was up to but he was back, quick as a flash, with a cup of scalding hot tea. "I put two sugars in it," he says, "You've had a shock, but get that down you and you'll be grand in minute or two."'

My lovely Brew. It was just like him. Seeing someone who needed help and not stopping to ask who they were or where they came from. My heart swelled as Meg went on, still clutching the open album.

'I barely had time to say thank you. He went back to his place near the bench that he'd set me up on and started singing, and this time I listened. And I couldn't stop listening. I sipped my sweet tea and do you know what? I sat there for half an hour listening to him.'

'Did you miss the boring meeting?'

'Sadly not, but I was very late.' She closed the book gently. 'Before I hobbled off I shook Brew's hand and I gave him my business card. I asked him to call me the following week. I didn't think he would, but he did. I took him out for dinner to say thank you and that was the beginning of everything. It was the beginning of my life, really.'

'Wow!' I said. It was the sort of thing you'd say about meeting your dream partner or having a kid or something.

'I know it seems odd. But my life is a little odd.' She smiled gently and held out both hands to help me off the bed. We both faced her huge mirror. I hardly recognised myself. Meg swapped her earrings for others which seemed equally decadent.

'Brew can tell you the story himself, but he was already friends with Scar and it wasn't long before we were all introduced. We'd meet up and talk about ways we could deliberately help people out and then sooner or later we just started to do it. It seemed natural, really.'

I wanted to laugh because I knew what she meant. Meg being with Brew and Scar in a run-down building in North Belfast, and all of them clubbing together to make some kind of Do-Gooder gang; it did seem completely natural now. Now that I knew them.

There was a knock on the bedroom door.

'Yes?' Meg said.

A man's deep voice. 'Ma'am, there are some, em, people who have arrived for you. They say they're here to help?'

It was the others. Meg opened the door.

'Thanks Freddie,' she said, 'Can you show them to kitchen?'

'Come on!' she said, turning to me with a broad smile. 'Showtime!'

It was hard to walk in the heels, partly because the carpet in the corridor was so thick it kept throwing me off balance. I followed her to the kitchen, where Scar and Brew were waiting.

Meg had to rush off and greet her guests but before long Jeeves showed up with Sara, who had just arrived.

'Laydee Sara!' said Scar, jumping off the table and kissing her hand. Sara laughed and gave us a twirl, the tiny little mirrors on her outfit catching the light. She was dressed in pink and turquoise.

'Wow,' I said, 'Your dress is amazing.'

'It's salwar kameez,' she said. 'I got it for my cousin's wedding. Pretty, I know. This is how my dad would like me to dress all the time.' She beamed and jumped up on the table with the rest of us.

'So, what are we singing?'

And for the next fifteen minutes we went through the set list with Sara and made some adjustments, nibbled on the white-chocolate-covered strawberries that Meg had left for us and jumped every time we heard a noise that we thought might be Jeeves coming to pick us up.

Dad had been happy about the arrangement too. He knew who Meg was because he'd covered a story about her charity work before, and he got all flustered when she phoned him.

'Oh, gracious, yes, yes indeed!' he said. 'Tilly would be honoured!'

Meg told him that I had been studying her work in school (not a lie) and that I had been in touch with her to ask about social issues (kind of not a lie) and that she'd been impressed by my moral attitude (maybe not a lie?) and would I like to come and help her out for the evening at a gala dinner charity event at her ginormous mansion at the other end of the country.

She didn't mention that she'd also invited a busking

squatter and a tattoo artist in a tux and high heels. He wouldn't have believed it anyway, much less that she was part of the gang that his paper was obsessed with. Meg had sent drivers for us – separate cabs for me, Brew, Scar and Sara. She said that she hadn't wanted to have the event without us. That the gala dinners she held raised a fortune for charity but she hated having to hobnob with the wealthiest people in Ireland all night without being able to let her hair down, and having us there would make her feel better. She promised to pay us all properly if we put on a decent show, and she knew the crowd would love us.

And they did. Scar had persuaded me to sing backing vocals ('Come on, Tills, it's more fun than serving canapés to Mr and Mrs Farquar-poo-poo, and I know you can sing . . . ') and he took the lead with Brew on guitar and Sara on keys. And Scar was right, it really was fun. I hadn't had time to rehearse, really, so I just sang the bits I knew and threw in a couple of harmonies where I was able to. Every so often Scar would give me a thumbs up behind his back, and we were good, properly good, like a real band. People were milling around in their tuxedos and evening dresses, drinking from crystal champagne flutes and laughing with one another.

We played song after song, hardly stopping for a breath between tunes, but instead of getting tired I felt more alive with each one, more energised. I looked at Brew and Sara and I could tell they were feeling it too. They weren't so much zoned out as plugged in – all of us, plugged in to one another, with Scar leading and singing notes so high you could imagine him flying above you. We finished with 'Black Eye', the song Brew had sung in the park, and when the first few bars kicked in I saw Meg turn from the person she was talking to and a huge smile break across her face. *It's like nothing else*, I thought, *to reach out to someone, just with music, and they join you in that place and you're all together. You see other people in the room, talking or drinking and they're ignoring you and it's like you're in a different room altogether. But the ones who are with you – it's like they're right beside you, backing you up.*

We stopped and Meg led the applause, right on the last beat. 'BRAVO!' she cried and everyone else began to clap as well. Scar bowed dramatically and then he turned and beckoned us all to do the same. We high-fived one another as we left the stage. Another mission complete.

Meg made her way towards us and hugged us all.

'So fabulous! I loved it. Thank you so much, darlings!'

'You should've sung one with us Meg,' said Brew.

'Oh, my dear, thank you, but I want these people to donate their money to the children's cancer ward, and if I sang I think they'd spend it all on taxis home.'

Meg organised someone to bring us drinks.

'Enjoy the rest of your night, and when you're ready to go just find Freddie and he'll arrange your lifts. I have to go and be the hostess with the mostest now. Ciao!' She hugged us all again and began moving away but she was still talking. 'I'll see you back in Belfast! Try the smoked salmon, by the way – it's incredible! And ask Freddie for a doggy bag. I'll check with him to make sure you did!'

And we did enjoy the rest of the night. The person who brought us drinks kept reappearing and asking if we wanted more. We did. Sara and I had one glass of champagne each and just Coke after that. Neither of us wanted Meg to meet our fathers on the warpath. Brew and Scar drank pints of lager and Guinness. We chatted to some of the guests, who marvelled at Sara's outfit and Scar's gel nails, and when they all started bidding on the auction items we went outside to explore the vast gardens surrounding Meg's home. We walked down the stone steps towards a fountain where a huge ornate mermaid, risen half out of the pond, poured water from a pail into the pond. Sitting on the edge of the fountain, we talked about Meg and her house and her double life.

'It's like she's a kind of superhero,' said Sara. 'Millionaire posh nob by day, anarchist punk by night.'

'Like Batman,' said Scar dreamily.

'Wha? Batman isn't an anarchist,' said Brew. 'The Joker – he's the anarchist.'

'But the Joker's bad,' I said. 'And Meg can't be the Joker. Her make-up is totally on fleek.'

Sara laughed. 'Yeah, the Joker could really use a hand with his lipstick skills.'

I giggled. 'But he's an anarchist punk? Maybe he missed his gob with the lippy on purpose as a critique of feminine beauty standards?'

'That does sound exactly like the Joker,' said Scar.

'Anyway,' said Brew, 'the point is, Batman might have a fancy suit and car and all, but he's still pure establishment through and through – he's an agent of the state in some ways, in fact ...'

'Oh, *shuttup* or I'll toss you in the pond,' slurred Scar,

pretending to lunge at Brew, who almost fell in as he jumped out of the way.

'Twatman!' sang Brew. 'That's what he is! Da na na na na na na na, TWATMAN!'

Scar got up and Brew jumped out of his way again as he hurled himself forward and face-planted in the pond. Sara yelped and jumped up as the water splashed her dress.

'Arrgghhh! It's freezing!' shrieked Scar.

I was laughing so hard that my chest hurt from trying to breathe and we were all laughing, and even when it was time to figure out how the hell to get Scar dry so that he didn't actually catch pneumonia we still couldn't keep our faces straight. We sent Brew to get Freddie, reasoning that Freddie would just think he was drunk and give him a towel, and that's what happened, and we spent the rest of the night trying to talk about other things but bursting into fits of giggles every so often, until we saw guests leaving the house and we knew it was time to get ourselves home too.

In the car, I rested my head back against the soft leather seat, more tired than I had realised, and I thought about what a thing I had found – a group of the best people, the funniest people, people who wanted me to be there with them. I grinned to myself, clutching the enormous box of goodies that Freddie had given each of us to take home. All that money and luxury, but the best thing was having one another.

'Good night?' asked the driver, looking in the mirror.

'The best,' I said.

'She's a good lady, isn't she?' he said. 'So generous.'

'Yes,' I said. 'I love Meg.'

And I did love her. I loved her for her openness, and her strange poshness, and her kindness.

'One in a million,' said the driver, 'Such a shame about her condition.'

'What condition?'

'Oh, you didn't know? She has a condition. Whole family suffers from it. Weak hearts or something. It's amazing she's still here, really. Funny, that, for someone so good, eh?'

# Chapter 36

'I don't understand this. Can you just explain it to me again?'

Dad's voice was quiet and sad. I could have coped if he'd been angry. If he'd been shouting at the principal, standing up and ranting. But he wasn't. He was sitting in front of Mr Lindsay's desk, beside me, the two of us like naughty little children, and his forehead was wrinkled like he was trying to solve a really confusing problem.

'On one hand it's quite simple,' Mr Lindsay said, his hands clasped and resting on the huge wooden desk. 'Tilly's grades have dropped significantly over the last couple of months. What is more mysterious is that nobody seems to know why.'

Both of them looked at me. I looked at the floor. I knew they wanted me to speak but I wasn't going to say anything until they forced me.

'Dropped significantly? What does that mean?' said Dad. 'How much trouble is she in?'

'Well.' The principal took a breath. 'The exams are in two

months. Right now, if things don't change, she may well fail them outright.'

I looked up then. Fail outright? I hadn't realised it was that bad.

'That's right,' said Mr Lindsay as if he'd read my mind. 'It's A levels, Tilly. You're smart, but you can't just coast along like you could with your GSCEs.'

Silence.

I wanted to care more. I wanted to feel more regret. But my head was still full of Meg. How could I think about exams and 'my future' when she might not have one at all? I wondered how long she . . . but shut up.

What if I could go back? What if I could jump in the TARDIS and go back and say 'Thanks, but no thanks,' when Brew offered me the coffee at the foot of Samson? I could walk home feeling flattered and think about him sometimes, but less and less as the weeks went by, and by the time I got to now I would hardly have thought about him at all. I wouldn't be sitting here with the principal tapping his annoying fingers on his desk and my dad fidgeting and trying to keep his mouth straight when it wanted to turn down. I wouldn't be so tired. I wouldn't be worried about the people I liked best in the whole world . . . because I wouldn't know them. I wouldn't be thinking about Brew and the people who wanted to beat him to a pulp, or Meg and her defective heart. These people, who were so brave but who lived on the edge and who made you love them so that it felt like you lived on the edge with them, even if you weren't in the same danger as them . . .

But I couldn't go back. I was here, in this office, with two adult men waiting for me to promise to make everything right again. And as much as I wanted to explain how impossible that was, at the same time I felt like laughing when I thought of Scar in the pond, and Brew yelling 'Twatman!', and then I wanted to cry when I thought about Meg and how she looked at me as we faced the mirror in her room.

It had always just been me and Dad. For as long as I could remember. How can you miss a person you never knew? But I did. And Meg made me feel like Mum was somehow there. I wondered if Brew felt like that too. And I knew he did. I wanted to call Meg up and tell her not to disappear. To stay in her mansion. To stop hanging around in damp squats, to stop running from the police in the dark, to stop clambering up on top of shelters to play music to violent kids. But it would have been useless. Most of all because I knew that they were who they were because of what they did, and that that's why I loved them. And that's why I was here, in the principal's office.

'Well,' said Dad, finally, flexing his hands and clasping them together again. His voice was steady and low. 'What's this all about, Tilly? You've been telling me you're working. Spending evenings in your room. Are you struggling with the work, is that it?'

I didn't know what to say. But I didn't have to say anything because the text tone on my phone sounded so loudly that everyone jumped.

'Who's that?' said Dad.

I knew who it was.

'Don't know.'

208

'Well, everyone's in class now, aren't they?'

I nodded.

'So, have you been texting in class? Is that what this is all about? Are you texting someone the whole time you're meant to have been working?'

I shook my head. I knew what was about to happen and there was nothing I could do to stop it.

'Let's see, then?'

Dad held out his hand. I looked at his face, calm and stern and looking back at mine, about to crumble.

He raised his eyebrows.

'It's nobody,' I said, blinking away tears.

'Well, if it's nobody, then you won't mind me having a look.'

I had no choice. I handed him the phone and returned my gaze to the carpet.

'So,' he said, after a minute. 'Who is *Brew*?'

'Nobody,' I whispered.

'You've got quite a few texts from Mr Nobody, haven't you?'

Silence.

I heard Dad breathing in slowly and then exhaling. His chair thudded lightly on the carpet as he got up. I looked up. He held out his hand to the principal.

'Thank you, Mr Lindsay, very much, for bringing this to my attention. I think we might have found the root of the problem. Tilly and I have some talking to do, and I can assure you, her work will return to its normal high standard as soon as possible.'

Mr Lindsay got up as well and shook Dad's hand.

'She will need some help catching up,' the principal said. 'Just let us know and we can arrange to have Tilly meet with her teachers to sort this out. I'm pleased we can help.' He turned to me then and nodded. 'This is your best chance, Tilly. We all want to see you succeed. Don't let yourself down.'

At home, the interrogation did not take long. I cried, Dad shouted, we both calmed down. We sat in the kitchen and he made tea. I told him parts of the truth: yes, Brew was my boyfriend. Yes, I had been spending time with him rather than studying. No, he did not go to the school. No, he was not an adult. No, he did not own a car or a house, he was not married, he did not have children, we were not sleeping together ... All the things you never ever want your dad to ask you about ... But there was one last thing, and I was hoping that he would have forgotten, but of course he hadn't, and I suppose he had been waiting to ask me because he was dreading the answer. 'This "Brew".' He made the name sound like something you'd call a thief or some other low life. 'Is he in that gang?'

'What gang?' I asked, looking at my mug of tea.

'You know what gang. That gang who you were with that night – the ones who trashed that play park. The ones going around Belfast making trouble.' I thought about lying but I could tell from his face that he had already figured it out and that pretending Brew wasn't in the gang would only make everything worse at this stage.

I nodded. 'But it's not like you think ...'

He had his eyes closed.

'You promised me,' he whispered.

It was hard to tell if he was angry or sad or a mixture of both. I only knew that I was in the biggest trouble of my life. That if I survived this conversation he was going to make it so hard for me to see Brew again. That he might even try to get him arrested. I wanted to be calm and think about what to say and think about what to do, but, sitting there, drinking lukewarm tea, I knew there was nothing. I was stuck fast to my father's discovery, and he wasn't going to let me out of his sight, not for a long time. I bowed my head and I said what I had to say.

'I'm sorry, Dad. I am, really, really sorry.'

And I was. Sorry that I had betrayed him, and sorry that he would never, could never, believe the truth. I was sorry he had found out because the principal had called him and suggested an urgent meeting. I was sorry I'd been stupid enough to think he would never notice.

I still had the phone in my pocket but I knew he'd take it away as part of my imprisonment. I wondered if he would forget for long enough to allow me to read Brew's text and text him back. I soon found out.

'Tilly. Look at me.'

He was sitting opposite me. His face looked so stony that it seemed he would never smile again. I wondered if anything would ever get back to normal. I doubted it.

'You've made a mistake. A big one,' he said in a softer tone than I had expected. 'But we're going to sort it now. You won't like it, but you will thank me when you're at university.'

'What are you going to do?' I asked.

'Put your phone on the table here, and bring your laptop downstairs. I'm going to cook the dinner and you're going to stay in your room until it's done, and I'm going to think about how we're going to sort this out. And then I'll let you know.'

# Chapter 37

These are the rules my dad imposed, to be reviewed (*'Reviewed,'* he stressed. 'Not abandoned.') after the exams were done:

Phone confiscated. I could use the home phone, with supervision, if I needed to call Beth.

No going out on week nights or at the weekends. No exceptions.

In case it wasn't 100 per cent clear already: no seeing Brew or 'that gang of hoodies', ever again.

Dad would call the school once a week to see if my work was improving.

The school would put me 'on report', like they did for the little kids, so that in every class I went to the teacher had to sign a form to say that I was present and working hard. Each day I would bring the form home for Dad to see.

And I was to tell him everything I knew about the gang, what Brew's real name was, where he lived. Everything.

'I don't know his real name,' I had said.

'I find that hard to believe,' he replied.

He was going to find everything hard to believe from now on, but I was going to do everything I could to protect Brew and the gang. It was the least I could do.

I stretched out on my bed. They'd be wondering where I'd disappeared to. Brew would be wondering if it was something he did. The worst thing was not being able to say goodbye. No, it wasn't. The worst thing was not seeing them any more. Being cut off. They were friends but they were like family now too. I don't think Dad could understand that.

I sat up. My head was thumping. I had cried myself to sleep and now I felt like a train had run over my face. My eyes were itchy and burning. I went to the bathroom and caught sight of myself in the mirror. Eyelids so swollen and body so sore that it seemed like I'd been in a physical fight. I let the cold tap run while I brushed my hair away from my face and grabbed an elastic to tie it back. Grim. I put my hand under the freezing water and splashed it onto my face. It hurt. I did it again. And again. Eyes slightly less puffy. It would have to do. With a bit of foundation I might look half-normal.

Dad was there when I went downstairs. He half-smiled. He was trying to make things OK again, but I knew him well enough to know that the rules were still going to be the rules, for a really long time. There wasn't much point in fighting it. On one hand, he was making sure that I was completely miserable – taking away my friends, Brew, my freedom. But I knew he couldn't ever understand that, and that this punishment was going to last until he could trust me again, and that that would be a very long time and if I refused to comply it would only make it longer.

So I half-smiled back. It made me want to cry again. Why couldn't he understand how things really were? OK, I had messed up with the school work, big time, but that was it. I hadn't actually done anything wrong. Well, not that he knew about anyway. I knew it wasn't legal to go breaking into derelict prisons. But it wasn't harming anyone. And my friends were good people. Dad shook his paper and continued reading. He'd never let me explain. I'd always be a stupid naive kid to him, thinking that bad people were good. He'd never ever try to see it from my point of view.

I buttered some toast and forced it down. Day one of a long sentence. Nothing to look forward to but study and exams. I wasn't even allowed to go down the town with Beth. I'd have to tell her at school. By the time I was allowed out again they'd all have forgotten me.

I blinked back tears as I said goodbye to Dad. There was no point in crying about it, was there. There was nothing I could do. I was sure I couldn't risk sneaking out to climb, or anything else, and no doubt Dad would be on to Beth's parents to ask them to keep a lookout in case Beth was trying to help me. At least I wasn't going to be bored. There was so much school work to catch up on ...

At break time I met Beth in the playground.

'What's wrong with you, gurny gub?' she said, plonking herself down beside me on the bench.

I told her.

'Shiiiiit.'

'I know. Goodbye social life.'

'And goodbye loverboy. Does he know?'

'Nope. Dad's got my phone and I don't know his number off by heart. And I can't go and find him, or any of them.'

We sat there for a few minutes watching the little kids play football and saying nothing.

'It's really rough that you can't at least tell them why you've gone missing,' Beth said at last. 'I mean, it's understandable that he doesn't want you to see them again, but . . . '

'You think this is a good thing, don't you?' I asked her.

Beth's sympathetic smile fell away.

'No . . . I just think . . . '

'What? That punishing me for having a life is a good way to make me happy?'

'No . . . '

'I can't believe you're siding with my dad! You've met them! You know they're good people and not the spides that the papers think they are.'

'Yeah, I know, but . . . '

'But what? These are my best friends, Beth.'

It just slipped out. I hadn't meant it to.

Beth got up, looking crushed, and started to walk away.

'Wait! Beth! Wait! I didn't mean that . . . '

But it was too late. Shit. Now I really had nobody. *Nice one, Tilly. Push away the only friend you've got left.*

But what had she been about to say, anyway? She probably thought we were above them with our sensible lives and our nice middle-class houses and big cars and nice schools and dreams about university. I know that's what Dad thought. Why would his nice, neat daughter want to chuck away her privilege for a gang of criminals?

# Chapter 38

Time is meant to heal, but how much time? A month? A year? Three years? The crucial moment is the point at which you give up hope. The point where you say to yourself, *that's it, time to move on now*. The point where you realise that a relationship is gone for good. Two weeks doesn't sound like long but it is a long time when all you have to look forward to is history revision and media essays and the odd break for coffee – coffee from your own kitchen, not from the coffee shop.

I poured myself a mug of lukewarm coffee from the pot and flicked on the heating. I wonder what it would be like to live in a warm country where nobody would put on the heating in the spring. They probably drank less coffee. I cut myself a slice of orange Madeira cake. It wasn't a caramel square from the Ark but it would do. As I carried it upstairs to the study torture chamber of my bedroom, I found myself dreaming of a large frothy cappuccino, thick malt shakes blended with Aero mint chocolate, long lattes with the little ginger biscuits on the side. When all of this was over I would spend the summer sitting on big coffee shop sofas with my books, and in the evenings I would climb and climb. I'd cycle out of Belfast, as far as I could, and climb the highest places. For now, climbing the stairs was all I could risk.

'You OK?' Dad had asked that morning. 'You look pale.'

'Probably a vitamin D deficiency,' I said.

He snorted, shaking out his paper. 'That's what you get for living in Ireland.'

*That's what I get for having a fascist dad who keeps me locked up*, I thought. But I didn't say it. I was on my best behaviour. He hadn't asked me a question about Brew or the gang for a few days and I was hoping this was the beginning of it all blowing over.

I wondered if it was all blowing over for Brew as well. Was he rescuing some other girl who didn't need rescuing now? Taking her to parties? Probably. Blokes moved on, didn't they? Daniel had been going steady with Paula Taylor, the South African kid, since about a week after he split up with Beth, and even though she had ended it and said she didn't care I could tell she was hurt at how quickly he had moved on.

I opened my history notes. All caught up now, but I still didn't understand some of it. I really needed Beth's help but Dad wouldn't let me hang out with her outside school.

I closed my file and opened my media folder instead. It fell open at the notes on the Bechdel test and I thought of Beth and what she'd said about me talking about Brew all the time. I remembered the last time I had spoken to her and how hurt she had looked. Maybe she wouldn't want to study with me now anyway. She was right about me and Brew, though. Two weeks apart and I was still thinking about him. Wondering where he was now. I was catching up on work but my heart wasn't in it. I would pass, but I couldn't ace my exams like this. I couldn't care less about Napoleon or Hamlet or any other sad bloke from a book.

I resisted googling the Maze prison to see what I could find out about the people who had been imprisoned there.

My eyes passed over the notes. I took out my highlighter and started highlighting things that seemed important, as if making them brighter would help them to implant in my head. I checked social media and did a search on the #BELNINJA1 hashtag. There were hundreds of posts; the last ninja gig had been last night. I looked up the account that Brew had set up to instigate the gigs. He hadn't updated it since the first time. I considered trying to find Brew and Scar on other social media sites, but remembered that neither of them used them. I guessed that if he had wanted to contact me he would have tried to find me online but Dad insisted that I was impossible to find – that all my accounts had the tightest security and that I told him my passwords so that he could check up on me from time to time. It was useless. I was unfindable. And I couldn't concentrate. I drank the rest of my coffee. The cake was untouched and I didn't feel like eating it any more. I shut the laptop and shut my file and lay down on my bed, putting my headphones on. Fifteen-minute break and then I'd try again. I fell asleep instantly and dreamt that Scar was giving me a tattoo of Bobby Sands, sitting in his prison cell reading a newspaper with the headline 'Gang of Unknowns Fail the Bechdel Test'.

Dad woke me up, knocking on my door.

'Tilly? You asleep? It's tea time.'

Shit. I'd slept for ages.

The door inched open.

'It's OK, Dad, come in.'

He came in and looked around the room as if he'd never been in there before. He picked up the cake and took a bite.

'Hey,' I said, sitting up and rubbing my eyes. 'You'll spoil your tea.'

He sat on the end of my bed, one hand cupped underneath the one holding the cake.

'I'll be grand. Are you exhausted from studying?'

'Em, yeah.'

'And how's it all going? The studying, I mean?' He took another bite of the cake and I felt my stomach growl.

'OK . . . '

'Just OK?' He raised an eyebrow.

'Well, yeah . . . I really need some help with some of the history notes . . . '

'Can't you google them or something?' He waved his cake hand around when he said 'google', as if it was some kind of space age technology.

'Not really, Dad. I need someone to explain it.'

'Could Beth explain it over the phone?'

'A bit, probably . . . ' Now was my chance. I would risk making him angry and reminding him about the gang again, but it was now or never. 'But it would be much better to have her beside me.' I smiled at him and tried to look innocent and hopeful. 'Just for a couple of hours. It would really help.'

He stood up and left the rest of the cake on the plate, brushing his hands together and letting the crumbs fall on the carpet.

'I'll think about it,' he said sternly.

'Thanks, Dad.'

I tried to smile gently, although my insides were turning cartwheels and my heart was hanging out bunting and getting ready for a celebration.

He looked uncertain but nodded his head and turned towards the door with the plate and the half-eaten cake. 'Come on down when you're ready. I'll defrost us some of that fish pie.'

Twenty minutes later, the smell of molten fish pie led me downstairs. I set the table and made a jug of diluting juice.

'OK,' said Dad when we were both seated. It was the kind of 'OK' that was going to come before a big announcement. *Please let it be the news I need to hear.*

'I've spoken to Beth's father.'

Yes. This was good.

'You've got two hours tomorrow afternoon. I've decided that you can cycle to Beth's house.'

OMG, he was letting me take the bike? This was way better than expected. I had imagined a meeting at our house, under his watchful eye.

'Don't look so surprised. I'm not a total monster, and it's obvious you need the fresh air. And your teachers have said you're making progress.'

'Thanks, Dad!'

I couldn't help myself. I broke out into a huge smile. It was the best news I'd heard in a fortnight.

'Two hours,' he said again, pointing a forkful of fish pie at me. 'And Beth's dad will be in the house and he will call me when you arrive and when you leave.'

'Understood!'

*Beth's dad will be in the house. Not in the room that we're in? Just 'in the house'? OMG! We might even have a nice time. If she was still my friend . . .*

'And I'll want to see evidence of the work you've done when you come back,' he continued.

'No problemo! You've no idea how much this will help, Dad. I mean it, a couple of hours with superbrain Beth and I'll have enough work to do me for at least the next week . . .'

'Don't push it,' said Dad, understanding what I was driving at. 'This is an experiment. An experiment in trust.' He smiled flatly, scooping another forkful into his mouth. 'Eat up!' he said, nodding at my untouched plate.

I did as I was told, the whole time figuring out how many hours until I would be able to leave the house, on my bike, the long way round to Beth's in the wind.

# Chapter 39

As it turned out, it was sixteen hours in total. Dad had figured out how long it might take me to get to Beth's and if her dad didn't call within a set period then the whole thing would be called off and Beth's dad would drive me home. Bloody hell, Dad could have had a great career as a prison officer. You could tell he was enjoying working everything out, making sure that everything was still under his control even when he couldn't see it. But I didn't care. Freedom! Well, relative freedom, being outside, without Dad, and without my uniform on.

I spent a full hour picking out my clothes. It's funny how the things that don't normally matter become so important when they've been taken away from you. My best black leggings, navy Vans with the lime stripe, plain black T-shirt, forest green hoodie. It was nothing Beth would recognise as fancy, but it felt good to me. I thought about the glittery eyeliner and decided against it – Dad didn't need another reason to be suspicious. I tied my hair back the same way I always did. I didn't go downstairs until the last minute, hoodie zipped up, fleece hat on, backpack full of folders and books strapped to my back.

'I'm away, Dad,' I called from the kitchen door.

'OK!' he yelled back from the living room. 'Don't forget to get there as soon as you . . .'

His voice tailed off as I closed the door. I'd heard the drill four times already since yesterday: get there on time, get straight to work, don't arse about making fancy coffee with Beth's mum's espresso machine, two hours' solid work, come straight back, don't be late . . .

I went to the shed to get my bike. The weather had been bad and I hoped it hadn't been leaked on because I wasn't going back inside for a towel; I'd rather have a wet bum than listen to more from Dad blahing on about the Trust Experiment. I unlocked the shed, but before I could open the door fully I noticed something sticking out between the planks of wood on the shed door – the corner of a sheet of paper. I opened the door fully to see it from the other side. Not a sheet of paper – an envelope. Slightly damp but mostly dried. And it had my name on the front.

I didn't have too much time but I could make it up if I went on the footpath on the main roads. I tore open the envelope. The note inside, in handwriting blurred by the rain, read:

Tilly – Dunno wots hapnin? Mayb your dumpin me or mayb sumthin els like lost fone? Rite back – leav a note in this dor. I'll chek evry nite for a few days + then giv up. Brew xx

Oh my God! There was no date on it. I had no idea when he'd left it. How many times had he been back since then? Had he given up already? I looked over my shoulder and shoved the note back in its envelope and then into my hoodie pocket. Later I'd have to burn it. I'd have to. Even if it was the last thing he ever said to me, because what if it wasn't? What if he came back tonight?

The bike ride to Beth's was full of what ifs. What if he didn't come? What if he sent that note ages ago and he'd stopped bothering? What if he did come and Dad saw him? He'd kill me. He'd kill Brew as well. Or at least set the cops on him. I had to find some way of reaching him. But how? Dad was letting me out today, but even if I behaved like the best prison inmate in the world he wasn't going to let me do it very often. My mind was racing and I was racing and I got to Beth's house well before her dad was expecting me.

'Keen to start work, eh?' he said.

I smiled and Beth appeared behind him, grabbed my arm and pulled me past her dad and into the kitchen. The table was piled high with Beth's folders and books, and there was a packet of chocolate biscuits and two mugs. Beth grinned excitedly and I couldn't help smiling back, relieved that she was being friendly.

'Let the fun begin, eh?' I said, sitting down.

She poured the coffee.

'Yep! Where shall we start? Napoleon?'

'Sure. But, just before we do ... I wanted to say sorry, for ... '

Beth put her hand on my arm.

'It's OK. I was being judgey. I'm sorry too. Let's forget about it.'

I could hear Beth's dad on the phone in the hall, talking to Dad and telling him I was there, early, and seemed keen to work. I thought about telling Beth about the note and decided not to. She had been such a good friend and I really did need her help with the work, but I also hadn't decided what to do about the note yet and I figured that the fewer people who knew about it, the better. It had so much potential to get messed up, to get me in even bigger trouble, to get Beth in trouble if I told her about it, and I didn't want to be grounded for life, especially not now that Dad was starting to think about trusting me again. So, for the next two hours, I got my head down and gave the Trust Experiment everything I'd got, hoping that Beth's dad would notice how studious we were being and pass it on to Dad. It kept my mind off Brew and the note, which was an added bonus, and by the time I was cycling home I understood the history notes and was feeling pretty pleased with myself.

I wished that I could go off for a climb to think about how to respond to Brew, but I knew there was no way, and anyway I'd have to sneak out after dark and what if Brew came to check the shed while I was out? So many what ifs.

'Get much done?'

Those were Dad's first words to me as I got in.

'Yeah, loads!' I shouted, heading up to my room.

'You left your bike in the garden. You'll need to put it in the shed or it'll rust!' he called.

'No problem. Just let me sort this stuff out and I'll put it in in a bit.'

I dumped my bag on my bed, congratulating myself on thinking of leaving the bike outside. I started going through my desk drawers. Sticks of used glue, scissors, felt pens with no lids, old hankies. I took a pack of gum out and left it on the desk. No sign of any envelopes. Wait – a card I'd bought for Beth when she was sick last year and hadn't given her. I took the envelope out from the plastic. It was pink. It would have to do. I tore a page from my notebook and tried to compose a note:

Brew, I hope you get this. Dad found out I've been seeing you. He took my phone and I'm grounded. I only found your note this morning. You can't come round here – he will freak if he sees you. Leave another message ...

Where? It had to be somewhere I could get to every day but also somewhere that I wouldn't look totally suspicious hiding a note. Or ... maybe it didn't have to be a place. Maybe it could be a person? I wondered if Beth would go for it. I couldn't ask her – it wouldn't be fair. But how, then? Who? Or where? It was so hard to figure it out when I was stuck in this room. I closed my eyes and imagined my journey to school: out of the house and turn left, the whole way down the street, hedge on the left, cars on the right, past the post box, past Sweeney's shop, cross over at the lights, past the train station, round the corner where it was dark and the trees hung over the road, and that was it – school on the right. Journey done.

No opportunity to leave a note without looking totally

suspicious. What I needed was to be able to leave it in the dark, or in a space where nobody could see what I was doing – a completely private space, like when I was on the top of a building, higher than anyone else. Brew could think of one, I bet – he spent his whole life hiding away right in the middle of the city. Hidden in plain sight. But he wasn't here and I had to think of this one myself.

I threw down my pen on the desk. It was useless. I got up to go to the loo but Dad was in there.

'Just a minute, love.'

I heard the flush and him washing his hands and the click as the door unlocked. The toilet was the only private place I had now – no Dad, no Beth's dad, no 'just checking in to see how your studies are going' . . .

Wait – that was it!

I rushed back to my room.

'Hey, the bathroom's free now?' called Dad.

'Just remembered something important about feminist theory!' I yelled back.

I heard him gently chuckle as he made for the stairs. If he knew what I was about to do I reckoned he'd never let me use the bathroom on my own again.

# Chapter 40

Note to Brew, stuck in the door of our shed:

> Brew, I hope you get this. Dad found out I've been seeing you. He took my phone and I'm grounded. I only found your note this morning. You can't come round here – he will freak if he sees you. Write another note, put it in a plastic bag and hide it in the toilet cistern in the first cubicle of the new gender neutral loos in the train station. I really hope you get this. I'm dead if Dad finds it.

The next day was Sunday. I looked from the kitchen to the shed door. The note was still there – I could just make out the tiny sliver of pink poking through.

Dad popped two slices of bread in the toaster.

'Nice out, eh?' he said. 'Might cut the grass later!'

Holy shit! He couldn't! The lawnmower was in the shed.

'Don't look so worried! I'm not going to make you help me – I know you've got those important things about Napoleon and Hitler to think about.'

He whistled to himself as the toast popped and he spread it with margarine in time to his tune, flicking on the kettle as he passed it on the way to the fridge.

'The good weather makes everything seem a bit brighter, doesn't it?' He beamed.

*Please let it rain. Please let it rain. Please let it rain.*

'I think there's a cloud over there,' I said.

'Whaaaaat?' said Dad, squinting at the window. 'Och, that's miles away, could be heading in the opposite direction. Think I'll get a good bit of the garden fixed today.'

He ruffled my hair and sat down to his toast. It should have made me feel good. It was the first time in weeks he had seemed happy. All I could think of was how much my note was about to ruin his good mood, and my entire life.

'Eat some breakfast, love. Sit down.'

I turned away from the window and sat at the table. Dad handed me a piece of his toast and I took it and started to nibble the edge.

'You OK?' he said, slurping his tea.

'Yeah, I just . . . '

The phone rang and I jumped.

Dad got up to answer it and I wondered if I could make it out to the shed to grab the note before he had finished, but he wandered back into the kitchen with the phone pressed against his ear.

'Yes. Yeah. Yep, I can do that. No, no, it's OK. Grand. I'll email it to you later.'

He pressed the end call button and left the phone on the table, sitting down again to finish his breakfast with a sigh.

'Well, that's my Sunday gone!' he said.

'Work?'

'Yes. Big story, apparently. Needs writing up by the morning. John's sending the details through now and I expect it'll take me all day to get it done. Oh well, the garden will wait, I suppose!'

I inwardly gave thanks to the God I didn't believe in. Yet, when I looked at Dad, his good mood clouded over, chewing his toast a little more slowly, I felt a familiar tug in my chest. If only everything I wanted to do wasn't everything he dreaded. But that wasn't right either – he didn't know Brew and the others, he hadn't even given them a chance. He loved that paper and its headlines so much that he would never dare let it be challenged. And look how it was ruining his day, but he would still be loyal to it. I left the table feeling sorry for myself. When I looked outside, over to the shed, the note had disappeared.

Notes between Brew and me, left and retrieved at the train station gender neutral toilets.

Brew: I'm getting Scar to write this. He's better at writing than me. He'll read your notes to me too OK so no lovey dovey stuff (winky face). I nearly didn't get your note. I'd given up. But Scar told me he'd walked by yours in the morning and seen a pink thing sticking out the shed door, so

232

I came by just in case, and sure enough. I hope your dad's not giving you too much shit (frowny face). Anyway. Let me know you got this and then I'll write more. I miss you. Shut up, Scar. (smiley face) Bx

Me: OMG my dad so almost found that note I sent you! Anyway, we're safe here for a bit. He'll let me out again eventually but not for a while. I have to prove that my exams won't suffer because my grades were dropping. I'm catching up now, though. These toilets are pretty nice. You should consider using them instead of the scuzzy leisure centre ones. A superior whizz can be had in these bogs. (smiley face) I think of you a lot and the others (hi Scar!) and I miss you too (shut up, Scar!) and I hope it isn't long till I can see you again. T x

Brew: I didn't know your grades were getting hurt. You should've told me. I don't want to be the cause of you failing school – you're so smart. You need to go off to college or whatever and be a proper bigwig business lady (winky face) You know what I mean though – you could do anything. Me, I can't even read and write properly – you don't want to end up living in an old ruin do you? Lecture over. There's something coming up soon ... it's going to be amazing ...

but I'm not telling you about it unless you double, double promise not to miss doing school work because of it, OK? B x

Me: I got a B+ in my last history essay, OK? Causes of Hitler's rise to power. Not an essay about my dad lol. I might not be able to get out (because of Hitler). But I double double promise I won't miss any school stuff ... What's going on? T x

Brew: OK you need to ditch this note soon as you've read it. Some political memorial thing coming up – most likely there'll be a riot. Mega party at ours and you have to come because we need to discuss the prison. We've been back to scope it some more. But can't say any more here. Say you'll come to the gig? Everyone misses you. And why didn't you get an A in that essay? An A next time, right? B x

Scar here – Brew's right – we miss you. Come back soon. x

I stuffed the note in my pocket, a knot in my chest at the thought of them going back to the prison without me. And another party . . . but how could I even hope to get to it? But I knew I would have to try. A few days ago I had thought there was no way I could even get in touch with Brew again and now here we were, talking (sort of) every day. We needed to talk in person. I needed to know if he knew about Meg's heart condition. I didn't think he did. I couldn't tell him in a note. I walked the rest of the way to school clutching the letter inside my pocket. I knew I'd have to bin it once I got there, just as I had done with all the other notes, but it didn't matter – we were back, Brew and me, the gang and me; I had my friends back. And maybe a party. And maybe even the prison idea. For the first time in weeks I let myself feel excited about the possibility of something beyond school and essays and study. I'd think about Dad later.

# Chapter 41

Dad let me go to Beth's again to study the following Saturday. That was all – just study. I still wasn't allowed to go out and socialise and I knew not to ask. But when he let me out to study the second time, and then the third, each time was easier than the time before. On the fourth Saturday, Beth's dad forgot to phone him and he didn't call to check up on us and he didn't mention the lack of phone call when I got back. He checked my work as usual, but Dad was predictable – my grades were rising, my daily report was impeccable, and those were the things he really cared about. So I made sure that his Perfect Dad ego was getting fed – I was the model student, and to tell you the truth I was quite enjoying getting good grades again and feeling on top of things. But I missed everyone so much and I missed climbing.

At nights as I was trying to get to sleep I would go over old climbs, trying to remember them in detail. I closed my eyes and thought about the very first one: some scaffolding up on the side of the leisure centre. Nothing beautiful about it but it was the first time I had walked past something on my way to somewhere else and wondered what it would be like to be at the top. The second time I walked past deliberately and took a good look. It would be a challenge. But not impossible. I might try it on a Sunday after hours when nobody was around. I'd pick a dry night. I'd wear clothes I could move in, but nothing that could get caught. And I'd get to the top.

And that's what I did. Trial and error. At first, trying to spread myself out and then realising that what was important was my centre of gravity, not how far out I could stretch. People think that a fat person can't do physical things. And they think that a fat person will be easily seen. But those two ideas cancel one another out. If nobody's expecting you to do something, you have much more cover than if they think you're a likely candidate. Big Tilly? Quiet, careful Tilly? On top of the leisure centre? Nah. Not in a million years. What they don't know is that climbing isn't about being tiny or light. It's about balance and strength. And the more you do it, the more balance and strength you develop. It took for ever to get up that scaffolding. Looking at my hands and feet. Tucking in my bum. Breathing. Using my knees. And when I was at the top I knew that it was something I would do again and again and again.

And now, lying on my bed, I knew that some day I'd be able to climb something else. Even if it wasn't in Belfast. It was just a matter of waiting. But would I see Brew again? That was going to take more planning.

The notes kept coming. Every day, apart from Saturday and Sunday.

'You look positively happy to be going to school on a Monday morning,' mused Dad.

I beamed at him. It was true. I was positively happy. And positively determined to get to the party. It was on Saturday night and I would be there. Somehow.

I decided not to tell Beth this time. It wouldn't have been fair to involve her and I knew that some day she was going to get sick of 'me and Brew' for the last time. I hadn't told her about the notes. I had stopped talking about the gang and tried to talk about other things. Everything seemed almost as normal as it had before I knew about the gang. Dad had even started letting me use my phone during the day, although I knew he still checked it at night. Beth stopped asking me about Brew, probably assuming that I had moved on or was trying to. It was just easier this way. If I failed and everything completely crashed then at least it would only be me in trouble. I shook the thought of failure from my mind as I threw on my coat and left the house. I couldn't contemplate failure.

And so, on Saturday night, at 11 p.m., one hour after I'd said good night to Dad, leaving him to his armchair and his book and his Radio 3 tunes, knowing he'd drop off, I stuffed a couple of spare pillows under my covers and crept quietly out of my room, grabbed my phone from the hall drawer, down the stairs, and out into the night.

It was dark and cold and beautiful and for a few moments I considered forgetting about the party and going for a climb. There was some new scaffolding in the town centre, deliciously high, and it hadn't rained today; there would be such a great view over the city . . .

But I was on a mission now, to get to the courthouse without being seen. I pulled my black hood up and kept close to the hedges. The roads were silent, almost spooky, but for the odd taxi. As I approached the city I could hear it. Chanting, shouting, glass breaking. A siren. I began to run towards it. It had started. I ducked down the street to the left before reaching the riot and then into the clearing where the Rat bikes were parked, then over towards the broken window. I took a moment to catch my breath and noticed my hand shaking as it reached out towards the window frame. It hadn't been *that* long. Five weeks. But it felt like the first time again, knowing this was all wrong in a way – an illegal home, an illegal party, a gang of law breakers. But I knew it was right as well – a building where people came together, a gang of do-gooders and do-betters, fearless people . . . people who wanted me. People who I wanted.

'I thought you weren't coming!'

I turned back to see who had spoken. In the dim light of the corridor I could make out that it was someone, a man, wearing what looked like red women's underwear. And black tights, and high heels.

'Is that you, Brew?'

Brew threw his arms around me in the corridor. At the point where I thought he was going to let go he tightened his grip, and I hugged him back, hard as I could, until we both almost fell over. We let go, laughing.

'Like the make up!' I said.

He laughed, batting his mascaraed eyelashes. 'Meg did it. *Rocky* theme. Did I not mention it? I really missed you,' he said.

'Me too.' We kissed briefly. 'What's a rocky theme?'

Brew wiped his crimson lipstick from my lips.

'Aw shit. I can't believe I didn't tell you. *Rocky Horror*, the film?'

I shrugged.

'Oh my God, I can't believe you've never seen *Rocky*.'

'You'll have to show me some time,' I said.

We kissed again and I could feel him smiling. We ignored the people pouring through the window and brushing past us, trying to get into the party. I could have just kissed him and gone home. It would have been enough. But there was more, waiting just beyond the end of the corridor. If I had known how much more, I wonder if I would have left or stayed.

# Chapter 42

'You've redecorated!'

Brew grinned, squeezing my hand. He hadn't let go of me since he saw me. 'Yeah, you like it?'

The main room was glowing in soft pink and orange light. The dancing skeletons were still chasing one another across the walls, their bones now highlighted in silver, reflecting the shapes cast by the disco ball's mirrors.

'It's beautiful.'

It was a world away from the riot outside where, we would later hear, the word had got around more quickly than usual. More people had come out with bricks, and bottles half filled with petrol, old rags corked in the top, ready to ignite.

Inside, the music was livelier than the last time. Spacey dance music with a heavy bass which made it sound like aliens had landed and were up for having a good time. There was a wider space at the front of the room – the benches had been moved right back to the edges so that there was more room to dance. And people were dancing, wildly, and smiling and laughing. And everyone was there – the Rats, the goths with faces painted white and one who had a huge spider's web drawn from ear to ear. Some of them had on wigs which had long hair at the back and were bald on top. I guessed it was the *Rocky* theme. Scar, in a red mini dress and black tights with a silver pattern which shone in the light with the skeleton bones, was dancing with another bearded and tattooed man wearing a gold sequined boob tube and gold leggings. They looked gorgeous and decadent in the weird, warm light.

Outside, someone was banging on Seany's door, dragging him out when he answered it. He was swearing, saying he needed to at least get his fucking shoes on. 'All out. All OUT. This is a big one,' the guy at the door was saying. 'OK, OK,' said Seany, and he pulled on his trainers and grabbed the hurling stick sitting at the door.

The dancers in the courtroom looked like a huge creature breathing in and out, everyone pulsing in time with one another. I wanted to be there, among them, and then I saw Meg. She was right in the middle of the breathing animal, her eyes shut, her arms above her head, raised to the ceiling, moving in time with everyone else. She was wearing a tiny gold top hat and her silver hair was now pink, now orange, now silver again, framing an angel's face, her shoulders softly moving with the music; she was at one with everyone and still she was on her own in that moment, a world to herself, as if she was conducting the whole thing with just her moving body. *I should tell Brew about her heart*, I thought. *But not now. Not tonight.*

'Stop staring, I'll get jealous.' Brew nudged me.

'I just ... she, I mean Meg, she's ...'

'Seriously, Tills, I don't wanna know!' Brew winked and pulled me onto the floor. 'Dance with me, you sexy thing.'

'I think I'm the least sexy person here,' I said, wishing I had at least worn jeans instead of tracky bottoms.

He pulled me onto the dancefloor. 'Don't be thick. You're gorgeous. Come on!'

Seany said when he saw the riot he knew it was different this time. There were more people. People he'd never seen before. The cops were struggling, even from the beginning, to keep the two sides apart. Both sides were throwing stuff at one another and at the cops. One of the cops fell over and another went to his aid and a crowd of about five people jumped them and started kicking and beating them with sticks. 'This is mad,' said Seany to the one who had knocked the door.

'It is mad. We're mad. We should be mad. Come on!' And he was away into the thick of it, dragging Seany with him.

Inside the courtroom, Brew and I were in the dancing creature, breathing with everyone else, lifting up our hands and letting the music move us. And it didn't matter then what I was wearing, or where I was, or what Dad was doing. It felt like everything was just right. A handmade banner stretched across the DJ's deck read *Don't dream it – be it!* and I wondered if Beth or Dad or anyone else we knew could remember a time where they felt they were being what they wanted to be, instead of just thinking about it. Dad, constantly chasing 'the big story' and Beth, dreaming about the perfect man while she made plans for the university education she thought was going to make her life complete.

The music changed and Scar and Meg started organising people into a line.

'I'm not feckin' line dancing!' I said, heading away from the floor, but Brew grabbed my arm.

'It's "The Time Warp", you numpty.'

'What?'

'Listen . . .'

To be honest, it was a bit like line dancing in a way. Only crazy, and fast, and it had a move called the 'pelvic thrust', which was hilarious when you looked around and saw every-one – all the goths, the bikers, Meg, everyone, all doing it. It made me think of how we let little kids have crazy birthday parties and dress up and do random dancing for rubbish prizes, but we outgrow it when we get older. Except maybe we don't outgrow it, maybe we just stop doing it. Maybe we just stop knowing what fun is altogether.

All I knew was that this was nothing like that time Beth and I went to a nightclub. It was Beth's seventeenth birthday and that's what she wanted to do – go to a nightclub and meet boys. We both got all dressed up – Beth wore a neon pink cropped T-shirt (which would have been fine except she teamed it up with a red and blue tartan mini skirt and green tights) and I wore my least casual clothes – black jeans and a black vest top with silver stars around the collar. Beth was wearing tons of make-up; I hardly recognised her.

'I can't believe your dad let you away with all that,' I said.

'I can't believe your dad let me into your house!' she replied.

But he did, because he trusted Beth. More than he trusted me. He was always talking about how she was 'a sensible girl' and he was right, to a point.

The nightclub had been too dark, too warm and too loud. And the music was crap. Hyper-speed high-pitched dance music which you could only dance to if you were off your face. And we were offered the opportunity almost immediately.

'Want a wee blast?'

A short guy with a moustache and a gold chain. He smelt of weed and crap aftershave.

'What?' yelled Beth, but I had heard him.

'No thanks,' I said, pulling Beth away.

'What did he want?' she yelled into my ear.

'To sell us drugs,' I yelled back, right at the point where the music cut out.

A few people looked round at us and one girl giggled and pretended to spit out her drink as she looked me up and down. I ignored her.

'Close your gob, Beth, you're catching flies.'

She blinked and shook herself out of her surprise.

And the rest of the night went the same way. At first we were polite. *No thank you, I don't want any E. No thank you, I don't want to dance. No, we're not a lesbian couple and we don't want to kiss each other for your entertainment.* By the end of the night Beth was yelling 'Fuck off, spide!' at any bloke who approached us. Much to our parents' delight we went home early, both stone cold sober because Beth had spotted someone putting something in someone else's drink. We never went back to a nightclub, and I never felt like I had missed out on the club-bing life. I had my own music, which I played at the volume I liked with the people I liked.

But this was different.

'Want a wee blast?' someone asked Seany.

'Yeah,' said Seany. He took the pill without asking what it was. *Why not?* he thought. *I might not get out of this alive anyway, might as well enjoy it.* But instead of pumping him up, the pill slowed everything down. The shocking mass of colour and fire and sirens started melting into a soupy grey rumble.

In the courtroom we danced and danced until the mascara was running down Brew's face in tiny rivers and I didn't want it to end. I hadn't even had a drink because I hadn't wanted to break the spell of whatever it was that was keeping us all moving madly together.

Sometimes you go out and your night goes as planned, no better and no worse; it is what you expected and there are no surprises. Sometimes the night is a let-down and you go home wondering why you bothered to go out in the first place. I know that every time I went out with the gang it was sur-prising. It was never boring – I might have had an idea about what was going to happen before I went, but it always went beyond that, because these people always went beyond what you might expect. Together their ideas, their plans, their per-sonalities wouldn't let them stay still. They would always be the ones changing the game, making things different. They never expected that someone else might play them in that way, that someone else might have a plan as well – a plan to alter things so that they'd never be the same again.

It happened when the music was winding down. We had pulled out the benches from the back of the room and settled to watch a few performers recreate their favourite songs from *Rocky Horror*. I had my head on Brew's chest, eyes closed, his arm around me. I had one ear on his heartbeat and the other on Scar's beautiful voice soaring above us. I wanted to stay like this for as long as I could.

*I just need to sit down for a bit*, thought Seany. He didn't know where his bat had gone. He stumbled to the kerb and a brick flew past his ear, so close it grazed his cheek, but still in the grey soup he couldn't move any quicker. He sat down and people began bumping into him. He crawled along the pavement, cutting his hand on a piece of glass, trying to see if there was a space, the fight roaring like a slow lion above him, eventually resting because he could not move any further. He thought he could hear someone repeating something, closer to him, closer to his face.

'Hey you. Hey you. You're Brew's wee friend, aren't you? Lads! Look at this – Brew's wee mate's here!'

We were sitting on the bench and I put my hand on Brew's stomach so that I could feel his breathing in time with the pulse in my ear. He jerked up suddenly and caught hold of my waist to steady me as he got up to face a young guy in normal clothes – jeans and a T-shirt – who was standing in front of us, out of breath and with blood on his shirt. He was saying,

'You've got to come now! You've got to come out! The riot's gone mad and they've got Seany.'

And Brew was away, without a word – he was running to the entrance.

'Scar!' I screamed. Scar stopped, mid-line. The music playing on behind him. He tripped over his microphone lead and Meg helped him up. Both of them without a word running to the door, the crazy music playing on, the stage abandoned.

I grabbed Meg's arm as she ran past.

'Wait!'

She looked at me with wild eyes, tugging slightly, annoyed.

'What is it, Tilly?'

'Maybe . . . maybe you should let Scar go after him?'

She shot me a look of utter confusion. Why wouldn't we immediately think of helping Brew? she seemed to be saying. Why would we leave it to someone else? I felt my face burning.

'Don't be silly,' she said, trying to hide her annoyance beneath an attempt at a smile. 'He's in trouble. Come on, we have to go!' She shrugged my grip away and ran. And I ran too.

Outside the old courthouse there was noise. Like a scream, but duller, as if the person was struggling to cry out.

'Where is he?' I said.

The three of us stood for a second, listening to the sound of the riot going on across the street. People cheering, police sirens blaring. Breaking glass. Dogs barking from the nearby houses.

'*BREW!*'

'It's OK,' said Scar. 'He'll be fine. He knows what he's . . . '

But as soon as he'd said it we saw him. Near the trees. He

was underneath someone in dark clothes who was punching him, again and again. We ran. As we got closer I saw Seany being held back by another one. You could hear Seany yelling against the sound of the riot.

'Get off him, you bastard! Get the fuck off him!'

Everything happened quickly after that.

'Stop it! Stop it!' I was yelling, my voice breaking. The three of us were trying to get the big guy off Brew. We clawed at him, kicking him, but he kept on going. He was like a machine. Then he stopped. He stood up and turned to face us. His face was pure anger. You could smell the beer on his breath. His lip was bleeding and he wiped it with his sleeve.

'Brew!' I shouted, falling down beside him. He was moving, just about. Moaning. His face was a mess.

The guy spoke.

'Away t'fuck! Fuck off!' he growled.

Nobody moved.

'You feel like a fight do ye, queer boy?' he said to Scar. 'You want some of this?' He cocked his head towards Brew.

Scar was silent but I could see his fists were clenched. Standing there in a red mini dress, I'd never seen him look so angry. But this guy was even bigger than he was. And he was drunk and who knows what else he was on. He kept on yelling.

'Fuck off! Youse better fuck off. See all them cops over there? They're busy. And that leaves youse all by yourselves.' He nodded to Scar. 'Take your granny home, sunshine, and put some fucking clothes on, you faggot.'

And I knew the guy was going to take a hit then. I would have done it myself but I couldn't move away from Brew.

I couldn't even shout. All I could do was hold him and let everything else happen around me. And then it did happen. But instead of it being Scar, it was Meg who leapt forward. She jumped with full force onto the guy and knocked him down to the ground.

'Meg! No!' Scar ran towards the two of them, Meg trying to hit the big guy, her hands in his hair, pulling tightly as he kicked at her to get her off him. Scar was trying to pull her away and kick the guy back at the same time and then we heard it. A single shot. Everything stopped and I turned around to look towards the riot, to see what had happened. But it hadn't come from the riot.

Everything was so quiet.

I turned to Scar and saw him pointing at the guy who had been holding Seany. The man was breathing rapidly, a gun dangling from his right hand.

'Sc- Sc . . . ' I couldn't speak.

'I'm OK, I'm OK, I'm OK.' He said it like he was trying to calm himself down.

'Meg?' Scar's voice was soft. 'Meg?'

Everyone was looking at her, lying there – an angel in the dark, the creeping pool of blood, blackening the grass.

# Chapter 43

I called Dad from the hospital. When I took out my phone there were five missed calls. Four from Beth and then one from Dad. A text from Beth:

Call me. I heard there was a shooting at the courts. Please call and tell me you weren't there.

The hospital waiting room was full of press. People with cameras and notebooks and voice recorders, all talking to one another loudly, trying to work out the story. Nurses trying to herd them outside and them questioning the nurses, the porters, the receptionists. All of them ignoring me and Scar as we sat on the plastic chairs. None of them realising that we could give them the scoop they wanted. Neither of us spoke. Scar was wearing a long dark coat that someone had given him to cover his outfit, or maybe just to keep him warm. He was staring straight ahead, zoned out. I didn't want to disturb him because I knew we'd both break if we started talking about it. But I needed to call Dad.

I wasn't even frightened. It wasn't as if he could do anything worse than what had already happened. Ground me for ever. Smash my phone up. Lock me in my room at night. None of that seemed to matter any more.

The phone only rang once before he picked up.

'Tilly? Thank God! Where are you?'

'At the hospital. The Royal.'

'The hospital? Oh God, are you . . . '

'No, don't worry I'm OK. Well, sort of. I'm not hurt . . . Can you come? I'll explain when you get here.'

'I'm on my way.'

Without looking at me or saying anything, Scar took my hand and held it tightly. I wondered if he was comforting me or himself.

A nurse pushed her way past the last of the journalists as they left. She made her way over to us.

'How is he?' Scar said, his voice hoarse.

The nurse wasn't smiling, the way nurses should.

'He'll be fine,' she said. 'The police are here. They'd like to speak to you both. Would that be OK? We have a private room.'

*He'll be fine.* No, he wouldn't be fine. He would never be fine again. Yet the relief of hearing the words made me start to cry.

'My dad's on his way,' I said. 'He'll not know where I am.'

'OK, well, you can wait until he gets here. Don't worry, love,' the nurse said, the smile appearing at last. 'They just want a chat. You're not in trouble.'

'I want to stay with her,' Scar said, still squeezing my hand.

'That's fine. They can wait a little while. But you'll speak to them this evening?'

We both nodded.

I had something else I needed to do. With my free hand, I wrote a text to Beth.

**I'm OK, Beth. Dad's coming to get me now. I'll speak to you soon – promise. X**

Dad was less angry than I had imagined. I stood up, letting him hug me, letting myself cry into his shirt. He stroked my hair. He seemed taller somehow. We stayed like that for a while. I felt Scar get up, place his hand on my back as he brushed past us. I heard him saying he was going to talk to the cops.

I didn't want to break free but I knew we had to talk at some point. The nurse ushered us into a private room, and we sat on chairs which were more comfortable and she brought us tea and then I told him everything. From the beginning. Everything about Brew and Meg and Scar. The missions, the press stories, the parties. And I told him how Meg saved Brew. They hadn't even tried to revive her at the courthouse. She was gone before the ambulance arrived. They bundled her up, strapped her to a stretcher and took her away, and we would never see her again.

I cried and Dad cried a bit too. And then I spoke to the police and told them all I could remember about what had happened. They asked who had shot Meg and I didn't know but they asked me to describe them. I wondered if Brew was going to tell them, because I was sure that he knew their names, and I was glad that I didn't, because what would I have done? Told the truth so they could find those bastards and lock them up for ever? Or lie, because sometimes bastards didn't get locked up and God knows what they'd've done to Brew if they thought I'd told? I understood now. How the group had protected me from this moment.

As we were leaving, Dad with his arm around me, we saw Scar and now Seany, both sitting on the same plastic seats. We stopped in front of them. Dad nodded hello to Scar and Seany and they both said hello back.

'Scar. Have you seen Brew?' I asked.

He nodded.

'He's OK, Tilly,' he said quietly. 'He's on a shedload of pain-killers so he's not saying much. But he's OK. Me and Seany'll stay with him tonight.'

'OK.'

Seany had his head in his hands. He might have been crying, I couldn't tell.

'I'll phone you tomorrow,' Scar said. He looked at Dad then. 'If that's OK with your dad, of course.'

Dad nodded, not smiling.

'OK. Thanks,' I said. And we left because I couldn't think of anything else to say and I didn't want to talk any more. I didn't want to do anything but sleep. I fell asleep in the car and woke up the next morning in my bed.

# Murder:
# Wealthy Pensioner, Elizabeth Mechtild Robinson-Fford, Killed by Gang of Unknows in City Riot

# Chapter 44

I spent as long as I could in bed when I woke up, trying not to make a noise, wondering what Dad was thinking. Was he dreaming up punishments or was his disappointment in me so deep that he was lying awake wondering where his good daughter had disappeared to? Every so often I remembered about Meg. Gone. So alive last night, and then ... How can a person, a whole life, a whole *story*, just stop like that? It was like being in a dream and everything being so real and complete and then you wake up and it all disappears and no matter what you do to try and climb back inside the dream you can feel it slipping away the more you try to hold on to it.

Eventually I had to get up to pee, and besides that I was starving and I could smell the breakfast Dad was cooking downstairs. I wondered how long he'd been awake. I looked at the clock in the hall. It was after midday.

'Good morning,' he said.

'Hi,' I replied.

He set down the frying pan so he could face me.

'How are you, love?'

'OK. My head's splittin'. Have we got any paracetamol?'

'Think so. Sit down. I'll get it.'

God, he was being so nice. I wasn't sure I could bear it.

I felt guilty eating the eggs and bacon. Like I should be so full of grief that I shouldn't be hungry or something. But I was hungry. I had two helpings and three mugs of tea. Dad didn't say anything until I had finished eating. And then:

'Your friend Scar called.'

'Oh. Did he say anything? About Brew, I mean?'

'Yes. Brew did well overnight. He has a broken wrist and a broken cheek and broken ribs but that's all. He will be fine. They're keeping him in hospital for a few days to make sure there's nothing else damaged.'

'Oh. Good.' I tried to smile at Dad, hoping he'd take it as a smile of remorse and hope.

He smiled gently back.

'Yes. I'm glad he's OK, Tilly. But I'm mainly relieved that you're OK.'

This was it. The lecture and the punishment and the speech and the bit I really didn't want to hear – the bit where Dad said he was disappointed in me.

But he didn't say any of it.

He said he loved me. He said he hoped I knew that. He said he knew that he had been harsh on me but that since Mum died . . .

He was blaming himself. And it was worse than anything I could have imagined.

'Dad. No. No, no, no. Please . . . Don't . . .'

He went on, staring at his mug of tea.

'Beth called me, Tilly. I heard about that shooting on the news, and I thought God, where will this end? The riots ... those young people whose parents don't know where they are, out throwing bricks, and who knows whose parents will get a phone call tonight to tell them bad news ... And then it was me. I was the parent. Beth said she was worried because you'd been there before – at the courthouse.'

He looked up at me, his eyes red, the sadness coursing down his cheeks.

'Oh Jesus, Tilly. I'm so glad you're all right. I don't know what I'd've done if ... '

'Ssssh, Dad. Stop it ... it wasn't your fault.'

I reached to touch his hand and he gripped it.

'I love you,' he said, again and again. 'I love you.'

'I love you too, Dad.'

Neither of us spoke about it for the rest of the afternoon. We sat on the sofa in our dressing gowns and watched telly until dinner time. We laughed at funny shows and when they'd finished we changed the channel until we found another one. Somehow it was what we both needed. Just to be beside one another, filling our heads with something else, being close together. The whole time Dad only let go of my hand when he got up to make cups of tea or when we needed the loo. If everything else in my life hadn't been totally awful this would have been the perfect afternoon. But it wouldn't have happened if all the other stuff hadn't happened.

We had fish and chips for tea and both of us fell asleep on the sofa.

# Why Was She There? Family of Rich Radical Asks Why She Was Involved

# Chapter 45

I stayed off school for a couple of days and Dad stayed off work. I think he mainly stayed off to make sure that I didn't see the papers but I looked them up online. Once the press found out that it was Meg who died they talked about nothing else. *Meg would have hated that*, I thought. If it had been some kid from the surrounding area, if it had been Brew or Seany, they'd've let it drop the next day. But no. Article after article speculated on why Meg was there, why was a millionaire at a riot? Why was she dressed like that? Who killed her and why?

But that wasn't the hardest thing to read. The hardest thing was reading about what was happening at her home. The well-to-do visitors. Freddie had been trying to keep things private but the press found ways to get past him so they could publish details about the posh people flooding in and out of the mansion. Poor Freddie. The papers were speculating about her funeral – where it would be, which church, who would conduct the ceremony. And I knew I wouldn't be there. I knew I wouldn't be allowed to go. And that was what was killing me. It was weird. Apart from

Mum's funeral, which I couldn't remember, I had only been to one other – my great aunt Jean's. I hadn't wanted to go because it's hard – all those sad people – and I knew there would be people there who hadn't seen me since Mum's and I didn't want to be reminded about her. Dad made me go because he thought it was the right thing to do but I had been so upset by it that he didn't force me when our next-door neighbour passed away. I had avoided all funerals since then. But now . . . now I wanted to be there. For Meg. To be with her as she left for good. And because I knew she'd want us all there.

Could I ask Dad about it? Would that be fair on him?

I googled the paper's death notices to see if I could find some proper details about it but there was no information. Loads of notices for her, though. Even some famous people had placed big notices to offer their condolences. It made me laugh because I suddenly realised that Meg had this life that I knew so little about. We'd seen glimpses of it, but it seemed like she had grown up with so many rich and famous people, and of course she was rich herself. And none of them knew about us. We were her big secret. And I think she liked us more than any of the others.

On the third day, Dad gave me back my phone.

'There are a few messages for you,' he said, setting it down on my desk.

Had he read them? I picked it up and scanned the list. Three from Brew. Two from Scar. Four from Beth. All unread, although perhaps he had read the previous ones, who knows.

'Thanks,' I said.

'It's not permanent,' he added.

'That's fine. Really, it's fine. I know that you can't trust me now, and ...'

'I just want to protect you, Tilly.' His voice was calm and low. He wasn't angry. He had thought this through.

'I know.' I folded my legs under me on the bed.

'I don't ... I don't know how to do that really. I suppose if you want to sneak out then you will ...'

'I won't! I swear to God, Dad. I won't.' I meant it as well. I never wanted to see him looking so frightened again.

'Well, I don't want you to. I want you to stop seeing those boys. I'm scared of what might happen, Tilly.'

I nodded. Stop seeing Brew. Never seeing him again? It was hard to imagine. Even when Dad had banned me from going out before I knew I'd find a way. But now? This was for real. I tried to stop myself looking upset. Dad sighed.

'I've given you back your phone because I want to be fair about this. You can have it for an hour. I would like you to text your friends ... those boys ... and tell them you can't see them any more. I won't force you, Tilly. I won't keep you locked up like I did before. I can see now, that it was wrong. I can see it just made you want to rebel ...'

I shook my head but he continued.

'... Beth is a good friend and maybe you can forget about the boys and start to hang around with her again, eh? She can even come for a sleepover if you like?'

A sleepover. The little-kid phrase made me want to cry even more. I wished I was little again. I could just about remember Mum and Dad and me, all together. And playing outside with Beth. Sleepovers.

'OK, Dad,' I said, trying to sound mature. 'Thank you. And I will text them and I won't sneak around behind your back to see them.'

'I love you, Tilly.'

He had told me several times over the last few days.

'I know. I love you too, Dad.'

He left and I read the texts – all from the day after the party.

Beth: **How are you? Hope you're OK. xxxxxx**

Beth: **You weren't at school. Hope you're OK. You want me to come over?**

Beth: **I'm guessing either you don't want to talk or your dad has your phone and he's really pissed off. Text me as soon as you can.**

Beth: **Going to bed. I'll not text you again but hopefully see you at school soon? xxx**

Scar: **Hi Tilly. I'm going to give you a call. I hope that's OK. I hope you're not in loads of trouble.**

Scar: **Hi Tilly. I talked to your dad. He seems like a good guy. Maybe we'll see you again soon. But if not we know it's not your fault. Do what you need to do. We love you. x**

Brew: **Hi Tilly. Hard to text with the wrong hand. Are you OK?**

Brew: **Hey. Scar said your dad said you're OK. I hope it's true. I love you.**

I caught my breath. He hadn't said that before.

Brew: **Won't text more – too difficult right now. Maybe your dad got your phone. Anyway. Love you. X**

I read each message several times, letting their voices fill my head, and I wished they were all here now beside me, even if nobody said anything. Even if all we did was cry. I suddenly felt a huge emptiness in my chest. A cave full of hurt. And there was nobody here to understand it. All those rich people, all those celebrities, if they felt anything like this they'd be able to go to Meg's funeral and feel it together. But I was alone, and it wasn't fair. I wanted to jump up and turn over my desk and throw my phone through the window and rip up all my clothes and scream out everybody's name and smash every picture frame, kick every wall, break everything that could break. And I couldn't even do that because it would upset Dad and he'd not know what to do, because I didn't know what to do, because this didn't have a solution. So I stuck my face deep into my pillow and I screamed as loud and as long as I could and then I did it again, and again, a mad hurricane of noise muffled by the foam and cotton, but I could hear the noise, I could feel it; maybe they could feel it too, maybe Meg could feel it, somewhere.

When I couldn't continue I kept my face buried in the pillow wondering how deep I could sink into it before I stopped breathing. The thought made me feel better. I lay on my back, exhausted, snapping myself out of falling asleep. One hour, he had said. And I only had part of that left now. I began to text them back.

To Beth: **Hi Beth! Dad had my phone. He let me stay off for a couple of days but I'll be in on Monday. I'm OK. I'm not really. I feel like complete and utter shit. He's taking my phone off me again but I'm not grounded so maybe we can hang out tomorrow? I would really love to see you. Don't believe the shite they're saying in the paper about us. I'll tell you the real** story. Phone me on the home phone – I won't have this one.

To Scar: I've promised Dad I'll not see you again. I'm about to text Brew the same thing. I don't want to hurt Dad any more. I will be thinking about you every day. I'll be wondering if you're at Meg's funeral. I'll be thinking about us and the missions. You and Meg and Brew are my friends for ever. I hope you know how amazing you are. I love you. Bye. Xxxx

And now the most difficult text.

To Brew: I promised Dad I wouldn't see you again, and so I won't. I won't be sneaking out to see you, and I won't be able to text or phone you. Maybe we can talk telepathically. I wish I didn't have to flush what we had away. And I love you too. X

I hoped he would understand what I meant.

# Chapter 46

I got the first message from Brew the next day. Beth and I were walking home from school and as we passed the train station I nipped in to use the loo.

> It's Scar here. I'm writing this for Brew. He wanted to say this:
>
>     I don't want you to get into trouble any more. If you need to break things off completely then do. I've hurt enough people.

No! he was blaming himself! No no no! I hope Scar would talk him out of it. I read on.

> Anyway. They're letting me out of here today and it's the funeral tomorrow. Me and S and a couple of others are going but we're gonna hang back and watch it from a distance for obvious reasons. I wish you could come. It's miles away,

*near her home. The Rats'll bring us. I'll tell you all about it after. I'm sorry for everything. I'm sorry you had to get involved with us. Love, B x*

Beth would be waiting for me, wondering what I was doing, but I had to respond. I ripped a page from my notebook and searched for a pen.

*Note for B — you have to stop blaming yourself. You, and the others too — you've been the best thing in my life. I hate that I can't be with you right now. But this is better than nothing. I'll be thinking about you all day tomorrow. I love you. Please don't hate yourself — M wouldn't want that, would she?*

I folded it up and stuck it in the plastic bag and put it in the cistern. It would have to do. In a way I felt glad that I had made the decision not to sneak out any more. I wanted so much to be at the funeral but it felt good to not have to worry about how to make it happen. Still, leaving the toilet cubicle and walking out to meet Beth, I felt a tiny stab of sickness in my stomach. It was a betrayal of a sort – contacting them. And I didn't think anyone, Dad or Beth, would understand that I couldn't possibly just cut Brew off, or Scar. How could I? They had already lost so much. But as I met up with Beth and she linked my arm and started happily chatting about the summer and what we'd do after the exams, I was thinking for the first time about the future. How was this going to continue? Was I going to chat with Brew and Scar using the gender-neutral loos at the train station for months? Years? What about if I went to university? Would I be away from Belfast like I'd planned? Would I start to call them? Would they visit? And if we kept it going, what then? Would I move in with Brew, into the derelict courthouse? How would Dad feel about that? It wasn't long before I could answer that question.

# Arson Attack on Cherished Listed Building Linked to Murder Case

A suspected arson attack which has destroyed the Crumlin Road courthouse building has been linked to the death of wealthy singleton Elizabeth Mechtild Robinson-Fford, who died after being caught up in rioting near the courthouse a few days ago. The popular philanthropist was buried yesterday, just a few hours before the courthouse was set alight. An anonymous source has spoken to the *Belfast Daily* about how he thinks the two events were somehow linked: 'It couldn't be a coincidence, could it? She was killed there and then it was burnt up. Perhaps there was some evidence inside?' Forensic teams are currently investigating ...

# Chapter 47

I ran to the train station. I didn't care if it looked suspicious. It felt good to run and I needed to get there before my brain completed the awful thoughts it was having. Where was Brew? When did he get back from the funeral? Was he safe? Was he . . . ?

I tore open the plastic bag.

I'm OK.

Scar's writing. Shakier than before.

Don't worry. I'm staying with Scar. We're all fine. The funeral was shit. Shitty shitty shit. All posh nobs and rich wankers giving speeches about how they didn't know why she was at the riot but that she was always an upstanding citizen and had done so much for the country. As if being there was a mistake. I swear, I wanted to run up

to the front of the church and grab the mic and
tell everyone what she was really like. None of
them know! Anyway. We kept to the back. She
was cremated. Her ashes will go to someone who
doesn't even know her, T, not like we do. Nobody
knew her like us. Got to go. Please write back. I
wish I could see you. I wish you were here. B x

Oh God, oh God. He was OK. But they were out to get
him. They'd burned down the whole building. The whole
massive building. Just to scare him. Or to kill him. How long
before they found him at Scar's? My mind started playing out
a scenario that I tried to stamp out. Brew's funeral. How many
people would be there? How would I get to it? Who would
pay for it? Shut up. Shut up! It couldn't happen, but I knew I
couldn't keep him safe either. The gang was breaking and there
was nobody on a mission to save us.

# Chapter 48

'Are you going to tell me what this is all about, then?'

Dad hadn't even sat down yet. He lowered himself into the chair, back to the wall, casting his eyes over the rest of the room.

'It's a cafe, Dad, not an interrogation room, don't look so scared.'

'I am scared. I've no idea what I'm here for.'

'It's nothing bad,' I said, sitting opposite him. 'Well, not really.'

His eyes widened.

'Christ. You're not . . . are you?'

'No. I'm not pregnant. Jesus, Dad.'

He sank back into the chair.

'Well, you've brought me to a public place for a reason. Because you think I'm going to "freak out", or whatever you kids call it.'

I tried to keep my face straight. He was right, though. I had brought him here for that very reason and I wasn't looking forward to the conversation.

'I'm going to order. What do you want?'

'You have to go up to the counter to order?' He rolled his eyes.

'Yes. It's normal, Dad. What do you want?'

'A tea, please.'

'That's it? A tea?'

'Yes, that's it. Do they not make tea these days? I suppose it'll be about three quid for a tea as well? A bit of hot water with a tea bag in. Ridiculous.'

'A tea it is.'

I walked as slowly as I could towards the counter, staring at the menu board, pretending to think about what I wanted. It was no use trying to think about what to say to Dad, because there was going to be no way to say what I had to say without him 'freaking out', so I might as well just come out with it.

'Large caramel latte, a double chocolate muffin and a tea, please.'

Simon behind the counter gave a little laugh.

'What's so funny?'

'You, bringing your da here and then ordering enough sugar to host a toddler's birthday party. You in trouble? Something to tell him?' He gave an exaggerated wink with his mouth open.

'No! Shut up!' I could feel my face burning. I didn't want Simon thinking ... well, whatever it was he was thinking. *Why does everyone think that? Do they all think I'm doing it? Maybe everyone thinks I'd doing it! With Brew!* We'd hardly done anything. Not that I hadn't thought about it, but that was my thought to think, wasn't it? *Urgh. Does everyone go around thinking about me doing it with boys all the time?*

I lifted the tray and paid Simon, trying not to look him in the eye.

'Keep the change.'

He popped the coins into the tip jar, turning to the next customer.

I walked back to the table and started taking things off the tray. This was it. Maybe the last time I'd ever mention Brew's name to Dad.

'Spit it out, love.' His voice was warm. 'After everything we've been through, it can't be that bad.'

I unwrapped my chocolate muffin, as if doing something ordinary would make what I was about to say seem more normal, and less like something that went against everything I'd told Dad I'd never do again.

'OK. Here goes.'

The music in the background was the song that Brew had played in the street that day when I gave him my phone number. A song about people finding a place to be together in the peace and quiet. I took a sip of coffee and listened to a few bars before starting to talk again.

'Dad, I promise that if you say no to this I won't mention it ever again, and I won't do it behind your back. OK?'

'OK . . .'

'Here it is: Um. I, I mean we, Brew and I, and Scar, we have a proposition for you.'

'You've been talking to them?' His face grew cloudy. 'How? Did you take your phone back? Have you been meeting up with them? Tilly, I thought we discussed this . . . ?'

'Don't go nuts, Dad—'

'Too late! You've already gone behind my back!'

'Wait. Sit down, Dad. Hear me out. Please.'

He glanced round. A couple at the table next to us were looking over. He sat down again.

'This had better be good,' he whispered.

'Brew sent me a note. I didn't sneak my phone, I swear. And I said I'd ask you, and this is me asking you.'

'Asking me what?'

'They're planning a thing. And it's a big risk, a *huge* risk, telling you about it ...'

'Is that meant to butter me up? Because right now I'm thinking of grounding you again ...'

'Just ... just listen. Everything the papers have said – about the gang, about Meg, about the shooting. It's all garbage.'

'Tilly. Love. I know they're your friends. But one of them is dead now. Do you understand how serious ... aw, don't cry, love. I just ... I just want you to be safe ...'

'I know.' I wiped my face with the napkin. 'Just, please listen, Dad. You can say no, and it'll be OK. I just need you to listen.'

'OK. Let's get out of here, though.'

And so we did. We walked out and the sun was setting over the docks and we walked for some distance alongside the boats bobbing in the water. It was cooler but not cold and the seagulls squawked overhead and one or two people walked past us going in the opposite direction. And after about half an hour I spoke again and this time I spoke without being interrupted, and Dad listened to everything, and when I had finished he said, 'I'll think about it,' and that was as good as you'd ever get with Dad, but I knew he *would* think about it, because we'd be giving him the scoop of the year in return for him helping us give Meg the send-off she deserved.

# Exclusive Interview.
# Gang Member Speaks Out About Murder of Elizabeth Mechtild Robinson-Fford

A member of the gang implicated in the death of one of Northern Ireland's most well-loved philanthropists has spoken exclusively to the *Belfast Daily* about the wealthy woman's involvement in the gang and who was really behind the murder.

An anonymous member of a Belfast gang who was implicated in the death of the landowner, Elizabeth Mechtild Robinson-Fford, has spoken candidly to the *Belfast Daily* about Robinson-Fford's involvement with the gang, alleging that it was not the gang who killed her, but a member of a rival group who killed the upper-class altruist unintentionally.

Robinson-Fford, owner of the Cairnslough estate, had, it has been alleged, been heavily involved with the gang of unknowns for months, helping one of them squat illegally in the disused courthouse on the Crumlin Road, which was burnt down in an arson attack last month. The millionairess also reportedly went on 'missions' with the gang to local flashpoints in order to try to quell conflict and help young people in trouble.

The young man, who gave the statement to one of our reporters, has alleged that Robinson-Fford's death was caused accidentally when the brave humanitarian got caught in the crossfire of a vicious attack on the young man, who had been in a dispute with another local gang. He has given a statement to the police.

When asked about his relationship to Robinson-Fford, the young man responded, 'Meg was important to the group. She took care of us. She wasn't our leader – we don't have a leader – but she was kind and she'd look out for us, you know? She brought me food sometimes. She loved the missions – helping people, being brave. She was the bravest person I ever met. She was always raising money for poor kids and inventing projects to help people in tough areas. But it wasn't enough for her. She wanted to know us. To listen to us. She always listened. I know some people will think it was some big ego trip for her, roughing it with the kids from the estate, getting a thrill out of getting chased by the cops. But the biggest thrill she got was seeing people happy. You might think she'd've been patronising or flashing her money about, but even though we all knew who she was, she was one of us. And we'll really miss her.'

The police are currently questioning two young men in connection with the death of Ms Robinson-Fford following a statement given to them by the young man who spoke to us. Read the rest of this amazing story in Sunday's edition of the *Belfast Daily*.

– *Belfast Daily*, early edition

Following the death of Meg Robinson, champion of peace and loved by many:

You are invited to an unofficial artistic celebration of peace and unity.

Every citizen of this country is invited to bring photographs, memorabilia and objects of importance to you to a memorial event in honour of every human who has passed on and who is fondly remembered.

You will be allocated a space in which to erect your memorial(s). You may bring anything of importance to you. When all memorials have been erected there will be a time of silence followed by a celebration of the variety of life which we have enjoyed and which we will continue to enjoy in our country.

Please be advised that this is an anti-sectarian event. You may bring flags, scarves, items of football clothing – anything at all which helps represent your feelings about your loved one. But please be aware that your memorial may be pitched next to a memorial which you find difficult to see. You are invited to bring peace to the space we offer, because it is a space for everyone.

Please bring candles, torches or lamps as there will be no electricity in the building.

We hope that as many people as possible will come and remember their loved ones, and that in the experience of remembering and witnessing the remembering of others, we might be united in our humanity, and committed to the living of lives which promote peace.

This is what Meg Robinson stood for and she died

because of a brave and selfless act of peace. May all those who have loved and lost join us as we remember her.

Maze prison chapel. 10 p.m. tonight.

– Notice in *the Belfast Daily*, late edition

# Chapter 49

It had taken Dad a week to think about it. During that time I
hadn't pushed him, but I could tell by the way he looked at me
that he knew I was thinking about it and that he was thinking
about it, and worrying about it, too. And then one morning
he sat down opposite me at breakfast, handed me a mug of tea
and said, 'OK then.'

'OK, what? You'll do it?'

'Yes.'

It was hard to know how to respond. I wanted to jump up
and hug him but he seemed serious and anxious.

'It's the right thing, Dad.'

'Is it?'

'Yes.'

'So. When can I talk to this Brew, then?'

'I'll arrange it. He's not exactly busy at the minute so I suppose any time.'

And we did arrange it. Brew came over, flanked by Scar and
Seany, who I guessed were his bodyguards now. They sat in the

living room politely drinking tea and eating Jaffa cakes while Dad took Brew and me into the kitchen to do the interview. It was the first time I'd seen them all in the fortnight since Meg died and it was so good to be with them again, but we didn't say a lot. We hugged. Seany looked the worst, black circles under his eyes. Brew held my hand for the entire interview. When he spoke to Dad he was polite and quiet and he answered everything honestly and when he said that he had been giving evidence to the police he squeezed my hand a bit tighter.

And then it was done and he gave Dad the note that they wanted him to put in the paper and Dad nodded and shook Brew's hand and thanked him for being so candid. And we didn't know what to do then. It was all so weird. Nobody quite being themselves, everyone being so careful, and all of them in my house for the first time. It was like visiting the queen for afternoon tea or something. What do people do when they're leaving the queen's house after afternoon tea? 'Thanks for the buns, Ma'am, better go and do the hoovering?' I broke the silence, taking a chance on the awkwardness.

'Dad, would it be OK if I walked with them all back to Scar's? I'll come straight home.'

Dad frowned.

'Hmmm. OK. But don't walk home on your own. Call me when you get to Scar's house and I'll collect you, OK?'

'Thanks, Dad.' I put my arms around his neck and drew him in. We were all being a bit brave and a bit careful, and in a way he was one of us now, and maybe he felt it too because as he showed us out he said, 'Good luck, Brew.' And I think he really meant it.

On the way to Scar's, Brew kept hold of my hand and Scar and Seany walked some distance behind us.

'It's so good to see you again,' said Brew.

'You too.' I squeezed his hand. 'I can't believe Dad went for it!'

'I know! It's going to be amazing, Tills. The Rats have been running us out to the Maze and we've almost finished setting it all up. You're coming to the event, right?'

'Du-uh, of course! Er, Dad's coming too . . . '

'That's fine.'

'Won't the cops come, though, once they hear about it from the paper?'

'Yeah, they'll come. But by that time we'll've decorated and we can say it wasn't us who did it.'

'I know, but they'll hardly just let a load of people in, will they?'

'We'll be there already. We've got a note written up to tell them we're occupying the prison.'

'Will that work? I mean . . . can you just do that?'

Brew shrugged. 'It's not a house owned by someone. They'll need to go and research the law about squatting and stuff. They can't just shift us out. I reckon by the time they sort out what they're allowed to do, the event'll be over and we'll be gone.'

Gone. Gone where?

'Brew?'

He knew what I was going to ask. His grip tightened on my hand. I didn't want to ask it, but I had to.

'Yeah?'

'What you said, to Dad, about talking to the cops and telling them who killed . . . '

'Yeah. I did it yesterday.'

'What . . . what's going to happen?'

'They'll put away the ones who did it, I suppose.' He shrugged again, but I knew that both of us knew it wasn't going to be that simple.

'And you'll be a tout.'

'Tilly.' He put his arm around my shoulder, but he was looking away from me. 'They already want me dead.' I slipped my arm around his waist. 'This way at least I get police protection.'

'What do you mean, police protection? Are they going to give you armed guards or something?' It was a joke but he didn't laugh.

'Something like that.'

'What? What do you mean?'

'Look.' He nodded towards the end of the street. 'We're nearly at Scar's place. And I want to have this moment with you. Can we talk about it tomorrow night? Please?'

'Sure.'

I rested my head on his shoulder and we walked that way, holding one another up, until we got to Scar's house.

# Chapter 50

'Dad, stop changing the radio channel!'

It came out slightly more forcefully than I had meant it to but he was doing my head in, flicking through the channels like a possessed man who knew he could never find the channel which would make him feel better about driving his daughter to an illegally occupied prison where a gang of freaks in weird outfits were waiting with home-brewed beer and spray cans.

He gripped the wheel tightly and looked at his watch again.

The paper had been out for a few hours. It was almost ten. His editor had agreed to run the ad on the condition that they prefaced it with a warning about how the gathering was not lawful and that the paper did not endorse anyone's attendance at the event. Dad said he knew that there would be trouble over it, especially if there was any trouble at the event, but his editor's point of view was that it was easier to apologise for something than to ask permission, and they wanted the story. They were waiting for the day after the event to print the rest of Brew's story, the one I had listened to him recount in the kitchen. The story about his mum, about meeting Meg, about the parties and the missions and the gang who beat him up and left him for dead. And about me. He'd talked about me. But Dad made sure that all mention of me was edited out.

When we got to the venue, the police were at the gate. Dad rolled down the window to speak to them but they just nodded and let him drive through. I couldn't believe it. Brew was right – they were just letting people in. Inside the gates there were lines of armoured police Land Rovers and bunches of cops, five or six at a time, standing around talking to one another with flak jackets, helmets and holding rifles.

'Bloody hell,' I said.

'Well, you can't blame them,' said Dad. 'Reading that ad in the paper. It's like an invitation to a riot, isn't it?'

'*No!* No, it isn't!'

'Sorreeee, I'm just saying . . .'

'Well, don't.'

I knew my tone was pushing it, after everything Dad had gone through. And I knew I should be grateful that he was here with me, looking out for me. And I knew he had a point, really. Even though the gang's intentions were good, you couldn't stop people showing up and making it into something else, could you? But still . . .

'Looks like this is it,' said Dad, pulling up beside the chapel building. There were police standing outside the door, one on each side, like they were guarding royalty. As we got out of the car, Scar and Brew came out of the chapel.

'Brew!' I yelled and as soon as he saw me he broke into a huge grin. The old Brew was back. He came running over and said hi to Dad and then hugged me so tightly it was hard to breathe.

'Come on in! It looks totally class! I can't wait till you see it . . .'

He babbled on about their letter and how annoyed the cops looked when they handed it to them, all the while gripping my hand as if I might wander off or get lost.

He bounced happily across the car park towards the chapel with me trying to keep up and Dad following us. Scar met us there and he threw his arms around me, extending one towards Dad at the same time to shake his hand over my shoulder.

'Hiya love, how are you?' he asked. I had missed his voice and his big bear hugs and thinking about missing him made me want to cry but I also didn't want to waste this opportunity to be there with them. Whatever happened, it was going to be a great night. I took Scar's hand in one of mine and Brew's in the other and we walked in together.

# Chapter 51

There was no music. Not at first, when I walked in. No sound at all, and for some reason it made everything that I could see bigger and more colourful. Like there was nothing to stop it all filling the whole room and filling my whole head.

Immediately in front of me, where the altar would have been, a huge wall had been filled with a painting. The head and shoulders of Santa Muerte. The massive white skull grinning over the room, her head covered in a blue scarf with a peacock feather design, and she was adorned with jewels and red and pink roses. She wore a bright feather boa and in each eye socket there was a portrait of someone's face.

'It's Meg,' I said.

'Oh my God!' said Dad, staring at the vast mural.

'Do you like it?' whispered Brew.

'I love it.' I turned to him, and we were both crying and smiling at the same time. 'She would have *loved* this, Brew.'

'I know.'

'Very impressive. And weird,' said Dad, wandering off to look at the rest of the room.

Everything emanated from Santa Muerte. Tiny Christmas tree lights, plugged into a portable battery, were strung from her headdress around the walls. There were more paintings: pictures of people, with their names written beside them and the dates indicating their lifespans. People Scar and Brew knew, I guessed. And painted beside each figure was an object or an animal; sometimes the animal was sitting on their shoulder or the object was being used by them. A tall grey-haired man with a cat on a lead. A beautiful fat woman with a parrot on her shoulder. A teenage boy holding a skateboard. Every single portrait was bright and so sharp that you could see the details, even with the Christmas tree lights and candles – green eyes, a rosy cheek, red painted fingernails. The chapel was empty but it felt alive.

'Did you bring something?' said Scar.

'Eh?'

'A memento? For the shrine?'

'Oh! Yeah. It's in my pack. Wait.'

I had brought a few things. A picture of Mum in a frame – one where she was holding me. I must have been only a few months old. I was crying and she was laughing. Dad told me that I always started to cry every time someone tried to take my picture as a baby and it became a running joke.

I also brought a scented candle from the hippy shop in town. It was my favourite one – black and smelling of exotic spices. And I brought Mum's necklace and a postcard that she had sent to Nana and which I took from Nana's house when she died.

I laid the things on the ground.

'What do I do with them?' I asked.

Scar shrugged. 'Take a space. Set them up. Spend some time with them. Leave them there or take them away again – it's up to you.'

I chose a space on the ground beside Santa Muerte. Nobody would notice my tiny things beside the huge mural and that was fine by me. It felt nice setting them out and I wondered why I hadn't done it at home ever.

'This is all a bit morbid, isn't it?' said Dad, walking over to my spot from his inspection of the murals. 'Hey – is that your mum's stuff? You didn't tell me you were bringing thi— hey, is that Nan's postcard?'

He picked it up and read the back, a smile stretching across his face and cutting the seriousness in two. 'God. I remember that holiday. Your mum got so badly sunburned on the first day that she had to stay in the hotel in a bath full of lukewarm water for four days.'

'I didn't know that!'

'Nobody did. She was mortified and swore me to secrecy.' He smiled and set the postcard back. 'She'd've been glad that her old mum never found out.'

I stood up. 'It's not morbid, Dad. It's good to remember people.'

'Yes, I suppose it is.'

He put his arm around me and we stood beside the small pile of Mum's things with the candle burning and watched the room begin to fill up with people. I could see Scar directing people, presumably telling them what he told me, and Brew was on the other side of the room doing the same.

'I should go and help,' I said. 'Dad, would you stay here with Mum's things?'

'Glad to, love,' he said, and he did something that I'd never seen Dad do ever. On the dirty concrete floor, in his work clothes, he sat down, right on the floor, in a dirty squat. I hadn't really seen Dad like this before – like a person who was something other than a straight-laced anxiety-driven news-paper guy. Now he had Mum's picture in his hand and he was looking at it so intently that I wondered if he was talking to her inside himself, and he seemed so much younger, like someone who did once have a partner, maybe like someone who could do it again some time.

I walked to the entrance and began telling people what Scar had told me: set up anywhere, take some time to be quiet with your loved one, leave the stuff there or take it with you, hang around or don't. Whatever feels right.

Outside the chapel there was noise. Cars on the gravel, people talking, some laughing nervously, men being loud. As soon as they came in there was silence. It was like nobody wanted to break what was already here. They set up their shrines all over the place, wherever they could find a spot. Some nailed things into the wall. There were flags. Ulster flags. Irish flags. British flags. There was a paramilitary flag. There were pictures, so many pictures. Photographs in frames, albums, even a huge poster of a soldier's face. There were signs written in Irish and English. There were objects: a policeman's hat, a football, rosary beads, a book, a hurley bat, medals – medals for war, medals for sport. And candles, tealights, votives; someone had even brought a candelabra. All lit in silence as people stood or sat or kneeled to remember. Time passed. I didn't know how much. Dad was sitting now, back to the wall, his eyes closed, Mum's picture in his hand. I loved him. I loved him so much for being there and for taking part and for loving Mum and for looking after me.

I felt someone's arms around my waist.

'I love you.'

I turned myself around into Brew's body.

'I love you too.'

We stayed in the silence for a moment and I wondered if, like me, Brew was hearing the echo of those words. How long would the echo last?

'This is really amazing, Brew,' I said.

'I know.'

'There's something I've been meaning to tell you. About that night. About Meg, I mean.'

'Oh?' His voice was quiet, like he didn't mind what it was. But it was hard for me. I didn't quite know how I would say it.

'She ... Meg, I mean ... I tried to stop her going outside.'

'Why?'

'Because I knew something about her.'

Brew stepped back slightly, still holding my arms. 'What did you know?'

'That she had some kind of condition. A heart thing. Her driver told me. She could have died. I mean, she could have died from *that*. So it was dangerous for her, to be doing things ... and I swear I tried to stop her from going outside. Maybe if I'd tried harder ...'

I couldn't say anything else. I knew what he'd say, because it was the same thing she'd said about him when we'd seen him in hospital together.

'You couldn't have stopped her, love.'

'I know. I just . . .'

He shook his head. 'It's not your fault. She did her own thing. We all did.'

We didn't say much after that. I suppose we were tired, and sad. In some ways the moment was terrible and solemn, and in some ways it was good and beautiful, and the room was calm, because nobody wanted to break it.

Time passed and we stood there looking over the shoulders of one another at the people and their memorials. And then Scar spoke. He was standing at the front, under Santa Muerte, and he didn't have to speak very loudly. Everyone turned their head towards him and Brew and I broke apart.

'Hi. My name's Scar. Me and my friends put the thing in the paper. Meg was our friend. She'd be so glad to see you all here. Thanks for coming. Death is a terrible thing and a sad thing. But, funny enough, it also unites us, because it happens to us all. I wanted to sing something, and I hope it's OK to break the silence. This is for Meg, and for all of us.

He began to sing, no music other than his voice. The song was 'Somewhere Over the Rainbow'. A kids' song. I remembered it from *The Wizard of Oz* – Dorothy holding her little dog and dreaming about a land where everything is good and nobody has any troubles and people's dreams come true. Brew squeezed my hand and I didn't look at him because I was crying and I could see that other people were too and I knew what he was going to tell me. I'd known it since the night Meg died. I knew it in the hospital and I knew it when Dad was interviewing him. I knew it this evening. But I didn't want him to say it. Not yet.

But then it was over. Scar finished singing and there was silence and then someone began to clap and then everyone clapped and a random guy from the crowd got up and hugged Scar and then another, and people were standing up and talking to one another and shaking hands. The service was over, and something else had started. And that's when Brew leant over and said, 'Can I get a minute to talk to you in private?' and I knew that he was going to say it and now was the time to hear it.

# Chapter 52

Sometimes when people have been deeply wounded by a sharp blade they'll say they didn't feel it in the way they expected to. The shock of it numbs the body, and they'll watch as the blood pours out, thinking, *Is that my arm? It's bleeding so much . . .* That is how it felt at first.

In American gangster films, it's called a witness protection programme. The informer is given a new life, a new identity, a new home in a new place. Somewhere far away from everyone they ever knew. In real life Belfast, it's a similar thing. Brew and I knew that on a certain day he would leave and that we wouldn't be able to see one another again. We couldn't write or chat on the phone. It would be a clean break, a total detachment.

We had ducked around the dark side of the prison chapel. There were no lights, but as we held one another I could feel his breathing, irregular, as he tried to hold in the inevitable, the words and the sadness, and then I felt his face wet against mine and then it was hard to tell whose tears belonged to who. We stood like that for a while, letting our bodies tell everything before speaking.

'So. I have to go.'

'I know.'

'I'm sorry. I don't want to.'

'It's fine. Well . . . not really, but you know . . . I know it has to be this way. Will you be safe?'

'Yes. But only if I don't tell you anything else about it.'

And that was all he could say, and I didn't ask anything else because everything was an unanswerable question. *Will I see you again? Where will you stay? How long does it have to be? How will you live? How will I live?* Even if he'd been allowed to answer, I doubt he could have. We spent as much time as we could together in the days before he left and we didn't talk about it, but every time he said 'I love you', I knew it meant 'Goodbye' or 'Don't forget me' or 'Sorry about all of this'. And I said it back, and it meant 'It's not your fault' or 'I'm glad we met' or 'Goodbye to you too'.

The memorial at the prison made the papers in a big way and some people who attended were interviewed and crowds gathered at the prison every day for a few weeks to have a look at the murals and the tokens which had been left. And in the middle of the excitement, Brew slipped quietly away, over the rainbow, to a land I couldn't imagine. I tried to be happy for him because I knew it would be a better life. He would have a proper house, at least. A chance to start over, away from the ones who wanted to harm him. I knew that Freddie had been to see him, to give him and the others some money that Meg had left them. But I knew that he'd miss it – the gang. I knew he'd miss me.

At least I had Scar. I called in to see him every day in the tattoo shop. Sometimes we'd talk a lot about Meg and Brew and everyone. Sometimes we'd just drink tea and say nothing. But it helped, having him there. I studied. I did my exams. I left school. None of it seemed spectacular but I was glad to have something to do. Dad and I started this ritual of watching telly together every Sunday evening, no matter what was on. And that helped too. I spent the two months of summer hanging out with Scar, helping him in the tattoo parlour. Just cleaning up, making tea. I went shopping with Beth. I watched TV with Dad. I felt the numbness, watching in amazement as the blood poured away, letting myself feel weaker and more tired.

In August, our exam results came. Beth and I walked to school together to get them early and because we decided we wanted to see them together. It was so strange walking on the path towards school. I thought about all the times I had walked it when Brew was here. I thought about our notes. As we walked past the railway station I felt like going in to check. Just in case. But I shook the thought from my head. He was gone. Had been gone for ten weeks. He had probably forgotten about me now. Or maybe not. But even if he hadn't, it didn't matter because . . .

'Hey.' Beth nudged me. 'You OK?'

'Yeah,' I lied.

'You nervous?'

'About what?'

'Du-uh, the results?'

'Oh. No, not very much anyway.' The truth was I didn't care any more really,

'Well.' Beth linked my arm. 'I'm shitting a brick. And you can stand beside me when I open mine, because if I don't get to Edinburgh to do Politics I'll cry. OK?'

I smiled. Beth would be fine. I might just scrape the grades for History in Liverpool, if I was lucky.

As we rounded the corner and saw the school I suddenly felt a heaviness in my stomach. Maybe I did care after all. I could see my teachers milling about at the school's main entrance. God, how was I going to face Mrs Matchett if I'd totally screwed it up? We walked to the school entrance, speeding up slightly, and *thud, thud,* there was my heart in my chest. It was good to feel it again. But what if I hadn't done enough? What if I'd just missed the chance to go away? What if I had to spend another year here resitting? And without Beth? Oh God . . .

Margaret, the school secretary, handed us our envelopes. Her eyes sparkled through her glasses and Beth beamed at her but I felt sick.

'I can't do this in front of you,' I said. 'I'm going to open mine in the loo.'

'OK. Well, hurry up, because I need you with me to open mine.'

'OK.'

I could have suggested opening Beth's first but I knew her success would make my failure seem even worse, and at least if I knew I'd flunked then I'd have a bit of time in the bog to compose myself and find a way to fake coolness.

Locked in the cubicle, I tore open the envelope.

English: B

Media: C

History: A

I stared at the little letters. What did it mean? I needed three Bs, not a C, a B and an A. An A! I got a bloody A in History! Holy crap! How did I even manage that?

*Knock knock.* Beth's voice:

'Well? Don't leave me in suspenders?'

I opened the door and Beth was wide eyed.

'Well?' she said, waving her hands.

'B, C, A.'

She gasped. 'What does that mean?'

'I haven't a bloody clue!'

'Shit!' She gave me an excited hug.

'I know! I'll have to phone them up. I might not make it . . . I don't think B, C, A is as good as B, B, B, is it?'

'I dunno! It sounds just as good. I mean – you got an A!'

'I know!'

'Oh my God, Tilly. I don't think I've seen you smile like that for months!'

She gave me a huge hug.

'Come on, then!' I said, breaking free, 'Open yours!'

Predictably Beth got three As – a sure ticket onto her course. It suddenly hit me that whether or not I got to Liverpool we'd be going in different directions. Maybe this was just growing up – everyone moving off. I wondered if we'd end up in the same place in later years or would that be it, for ever drifting apart? I tried not to think about it. Beth wanted to celebrate and she was right – I hadn't smiled for a long time, so I decided I'd celebrate as much as I possibly could, this thing which was making us happy and which might end up breaking us apart.

We went to Delaney's and had mochaccinos and chocolate cheesecake, and when the waitress asked us with a glint if we were developing a serious problem with sugar we told her our news and she told the manager, who gave us our glucose fix for free. Beth decided we should use the spare cash to get 'a proper drink' and so we went to the nearest posh-looking bar and ordered two glasses of champagne. The bartender raised an eyebrow but she didn't ID us and she served the cool bubbly glasses with a little dish of miniature cheese biscuits shaped like fish. We sipped champagne and giggled as it fizzed up our noses and we clinked glasses and made up stories about what our lives would be like at university.

'I'll have a super-ripped boyfriend named Giles,' said Beth.

'Giles?'

'Of course,' she said, putting on a ridiculously upper-class accent. 'He'll be posh as feck and wear a little peaked cap.'

'You're sick,' I said, choking on a tiny cheese fish biscuit. 'I don't ever want to meet Giles. Don't invite me to your wedding, he sounds like a knob.'

'You're just jealous, because you'll be in love with Michelle from Glasgow and she won't give you a second glance and you'll have to make do with Kevin whose mum does his washing at the weekends and who picks his nose.'

'Oh, charming!'

'Well, unfortunately it's true. And the worst thing is that sexy Michelle is your tutor and you have to see her every week, and Kev is the barman in the student bar so if you want cheap pints you can't tell him that the nose-picking totally turns you.'

'Urgh. Stop talking about nose food!'

'It's not my fault, it's Kev's – talk to him about it!'

We went on like that for a while until it was time to go. On the way home we passed the station again. I don't know if it was the champagne or maybe it was guilt for not feeling as bad as I should about entertaining the thought of Kevin and his disgusting diet, but there was something I needed to do.

'Back in a sec. Just need the loo,' I shouted to Beth as I dashed off.

I had to wait to use the gender-neutral toilet. It felt like for ever. *Flush*. It was stupid. I had stopped checking the toilets weeks ago, before Brew left. The sound of a tap running. There was no point. But I had to look, just one last time. The hand drier sounded like a rocket taking off. *Click*.

I tried to breathe slowly.

I looked into the cistern. There was something there. In the little bag. A note.

I don't know if you'll get this. But I hope you get to Liverpool. Here's to new life. Love, always, B x

I read it three or four times and put it in my pocket.

What was it Mr White used to say? Not everything is a metaphor. Not everything is a secret message. Sometimes a cloud is just a cloud. Sometimes the sun is just the sun. And in that note, maybe the words just meant what they meant – maybe it was just a message to say goodbye, to wish me luck and love. Always. It wouldn't be easy to hold the words in my heart like that – not hoping, not wishing. But I would try, because they were good enough on their own. And if Meg had taught me anything, it was not to miss the things that are right there in front of you while you look for something else; not to miss life, not to miss love. I linked Beth's arm and we walked home talking nonsense and laughing and I decided to keep that note.

On my eighteenth birthday, exactly one week before I left for Liverpool, I climbed the Angel of Thanksgiving – a twenty-metre woman in the middle of the city. In the dark hours of the morning I sat on her shoulder and watched the traffic pass, my arms outstretched to grip the angel bones keeping me steady, and I looked at the new tattoo on my wrist. A gift from Scar: a small 'x' to remind me of everything that had happened and everything that might be yet to come.

x for a kiss
x for love
x for a mystery
x for the unknowns.

# Acknowledgements

Much of the *The Unknowns* was written in Belfast and while it is an entirely fictional story I have tried to give an impression of the Belfast that I love: those families of birth and of choice who do their best by one another; those people who intentionally cross boundaries (physical or otherwise) to help people, sometimes to help strangers; those artists who are committed to truth and compassion; communities who look out for the humanity in those around them. Many of those mentioned below have been part of this experience of Belfast for me, and I am most grateful for it.

Thanks to:

Ian – *go raibh maith agat*, for everything.

Mags, Anto and Daíthí for pesto cocktails, fancy dress and tunes.

Anto O'Kane, for providing the lyrics of Tin Pot Operation's 'Black Eye'.

The Belfast Rats collective (and David Boyd for the introduction).

Ruth McCarthy of Outburst Queer Arts Festival.

The Dock Café, Titanic Quarter.

The Arts Council, NI.

Paul Magrs, Sheena Wilkinson and Claire Hennessy, for getting it, and for helping me.

Thanks also to Peterson Toscano for his friendship, wisdom and weirdness, and to my Animal Stewpots for the emergency readings and much laughter.

Finally, a huge thank you to my agent, Jenny Savill, and to my editor, Olivia Hutchings, for bringing the things I've dreamt about to life.

There are many more people than I could mention in one breath. *Ar scáth a chéile a mhaireas na daoine.* Thank you.

X